The world of
# FEMDOM

L D Hawley

# Contents

**Page**

**Intro** ............................................................................................. 1

**Prelude**

Pre-Virus ....................................................................................... 2

New Beginning ............................................................................. 7

School Life .................................................................................. 10

The Meeting ............................................................................... 13

Gain Access ................................................................................ 23

Exposed ...................................................................................... 29

Aftermath .......................................................... , ..................... 33

Virus ........................................................................................... 40

Reconstruction .......................................................................... 49

**Chapter**

1 ................................................................................................. 51

2 ................................................................................................. 81

3 ............................................................................................... 105

4 ............................................................................................... 129

5 ............................................................................................... 147

6 ............................................................................................... 173

| Chapter | Page |
|---|---|
| 7 | 191 |
| 8 | 211 |
| 9 | 233 |
| 10 | 247 |
| 11 | 257 |
| 12 | 269 |
| 13 | 281 |
| 14 | 293 |
| 15 | 307 |
| 16 | 319 |

Copyright © 2023 by L D Hawley

**This is the work of fiction. Names, characters, places, and incidents either are the product of the author's imagination or are used fictitiously. Any resemblance to actual persons, living or dead, events, or locales is entirely coincidental.**

**All rights reserved. No part of this book may be reproduced or used in any manner without written permission of the copyright owner except for the use of quotations in a book review.**

First paperback edition April 2023

Book design by Authors Issue

**Cover Art:** Lamonte Hawley

**Models:** Ilis Hawley, Lucretia Johnson, T La'Toyia Warren, Lavator Jefferson

ISBN: 979-8-218-18129-1 (paperback)

Published by Authors Issue

authorsissue@gmail.com

*'Some things are best left unknown. It doesn't matter at all about your reasons why you digging. Remember, anytime you dig, you guaranteed to come up with some dirt.'*

Fem Madam

**Introduction**

There were so many societal truths in the old world that the people became disillusioned with their individual ideologue truths. Identities were creatively adopted and replaced with gender free pronouns. The contaminants of that world eroded the very fibers of hu-MAN-ity. Even a large fraction of mankind rejected the genetic makeup of himself and preferred to be called fems.

For decades, the word man, male and other masculine attributes that narrowly defined what a man is, was targeted. There was even a push from feministic organizations that fought the federal government to expel any word that contained gender specific pronouns like; him, he and his. This push was gaining momentum. Organizers of this movement lost control when the virus swept the globe. They no longer maintain their grip on the narrative.

After being plagued by Chromovirus, the world finally got what they were asking for, a manless society. Twenty-six years without an XY presence. Who would have ever thought that women, who are called Fems in the New World, would survive? A world ran by Fems. I guess it's only possible in the World of Femdom.

**Pre-Virus**

Strife began to erupt from earth's core. This dissention shook the surface of mankind literally. Mankind was ground zero for this social eruption. This implosion was provoked from centuries of what use to be called gender inequality. The refusal of man-kinds acknowledgment of the woman's place, power and evolutionary purpose became the wick. Discovery of the Treaty became the spark that ignited it all.

Governments in times past were established on gender suppression through religion, education, and media outlets. Centuries before the Virus hit, our founding fathers hid a signed Domestic Treaty which possessed evidence that exposed their methodology of ascendancy through gender supremacy. This Treaty was hidden in a place called The Vaults. The Vaults were said to be secured in a secret area three floors under the Pentagon. Some say that the objective of the 911 attack on the Pentagon was an attempt to retrieve the Treaty. This Treaty was rumored to be sealed with blood and stored beneath documents from the founders of Eulogian Club, the Rosicrucian's and even the Freemasons scrolls. These pacts were intentionally developed into mythologies over time. The government conspired and deemed all that spread and uncovered the veracity of the Treaty as conspiracy theorist. This was done to silence their influence in the Old World, which is later called, The Undiscussed. It was also said that those that got close to discovering the location of The Vault were put to death along with their families. It wasn't until a young Archaeologist named Dr. Bethany M. Smith discovered these contracts and exposed its content to the world.

Okay, let me slow this down and explain who Dr. Bethany Smith, the person is. Bethany was born in a town in Texas called Hawley. Hawley was a small town of farmers. Her dad was a farmer, and he pastored a small church in town. He had two daughters. The oldest daughter's name was Jazmine. Mr. Smith was very old fashioned in his principles. He was very strict on the Bibles' stance on headship. Mr. Smith chauvinistically believed that a woman's place was in the home tending to the children and making their house a home. The only problem with his beliefs was that his wife died while giving birth to Bethany, so he forced his older daughter Jazmine to take on the role of mom and sometimes wife. Bethany was frequented by depression through self-blame because of this. Her dad was left with the decision of life and death during birth, and she carried the weight of his decision for the rest of her life.

His oldest daughter Jazmine was born deaf and was communally abandoned and lived introvertly. Though her mom connected with her by sign language, sad to say, her dad never learned that way of communicating. He communicated through the vibrations of his volume. She learned early after Bethany was born, how to interpret his desires by his disposition. Even his parishioners ignored his signs of contempt toward Jazmine. Instead of the church providing refuge and safety for her, she became a part of pity prayers from the women's group. The children of the church ridiculed her off what the elder's thought were private conversations. Being parentified and traumatized from the silent abuse that cried so loud, she succumbed to its detriment.

Jazmine went to church every Sunday early and made sure the church was clean and ready for Sunday school and morning services. The week before this Sunday, Jazmine seemed extra happy at home. The way she drifted around her routines and responsibilities resembled a butterfly breaking through its cocoon. Her entire childhood after her mom's death by decision, was spent squirming through life like a caterpillar. This week was different. She took the time and showed Bethany how to cook some meals that her dad required from her. Jazmine even began to teach her some basic signs like hello, goodbye, thank you, yes, no and I love you. Bethany was in shock. This is the first time that these two ever shared a moment. Bethany had no clue it was the last moment of their lifetime.

On the way to church, Jazmine grabbed some rope out from the barn. Because no one shared her space, no one connected to her emptiness, so her actions went unnoticed. She cleaned the church and cut on the furnace to knock the chill out before the members arrived. Her routine was to sit on the front row and welcome the attendees for Sunday school. Fifteen minutes before anyone arrived, she grabbed a small ladder from the custodian closet. She tested the rope against the strength of the ceiling fan that hung over the alter in front of the church. After a couple of tugs of the rope, she tied a noose large enough to fit around her frail neck. She quietly took a step off the ladder. Mr. Smith and Bethany were the first to arrive. Her best friend Amanda and her mom drove up. Bethany waited on the church steps to talk to her friend as her dad entered the building.

There was a male and female restroom at the entrance of the church. He walked in and made sure Jazmine cleaned each one. The trash hadn't been emptied and he was enraged. His volume shook the glass on the two foyer doors leading into the sanctuary.

   "Why didn't you dump the trash! Everyone will be here……….."

His heart sank as the solitude of the sanctuary comforted Jazmine's' lifeless body.

Bethany was about twelve years old when Jazmine left her pain at the alter through suicide. Jazmine's death not only marked the day that changed Bethany forever, but it also marked the last time she entered into a church again. Their house went unkept. Bethany was left to fend for herself. The church was closed, and Mr. Smith lived out his life soaking in a tub of guilt, regret, and depression.

Bethany spent the rest of her teen years struggling to connect to the world around her. She spent a lot of time alone and isolated from others' opinions. Some people find solace from life's trauma by self-medicating, but her place of peace was in the attic. She called the attic her heaven because it hovered above the pain and memories that her home conceived. The attic was filled with memories she didn't experience. There were photo albums and all her mom's belongings stored in containers. When she didn't have school, she would spend days playing dress up with her mom's clothes. Dusting off her mom's shoes and church hats as she fashioned her clothes to her taste. She also discovered that her mom loved old artifacts. There was a large plastic container filled with ancient documents, relics, and stones. Bethany became intrigued with her moms' hobbies. She found a container filled with newspaper articles and old books. All the articles and books focused on something about the Treaties. Out of all the documents and things her mom saved, this seemed to be her largest collection. Because of her broken relationship with her dad and the communication barrier she had with her sister, she knew absolutely nothing about who her mother was. Now she has learned everything she will ever know about her through the voice of the attic.

**New beginnings**

Bethany is a senior in high school. The summer before that year, she was welcomed into the home of her best friend from church, Amanda. Their house became condemned because of the condemnation Mr. Smith bore. The last time the home was cleaned was the Sunday they found Jazmine. Bethany was happy to leave and only requested that she would be able to keep her mom's things. Amanda's parents had no problem with that. They were so considerate that they even created a spot in their attic in honor of her mother.

Its graduation time. Bethany did not participate in any type of athletic programs, or groups in school. That was her way of avoiding people as much as possible. She ghostly walked the halls of high school as a loner. College was her next step. She was very book smart and finished at the top of a class that only existed physically to her. Writing became her first love after years of intimate moments she shared with her diary. Jazmine communicated with those that understood with sign language and Bethany language became writing to her diary, which was the only person that she felt cared what she had to say. She naturally excelled in math, science, and history. Universities from all over wanted Bethany. The problem was a lot of universities didn't spark her interest when it came to her course study. Her goal was to be an Archaeologist so she looked for schools that she could major in Anthropology.

The life of Bethany produced more tears than happiness. Even her closest friends and family could count on one hand, the times they heard her laugh or seen her smile throughout her existence. Nothing made her happy but her attic time with her mom's memories. One day after school, her and Amanda came home and noticed that Amandas' mom was acting strange. Amanda asked her what was wrong, she pulled her to the side and whispered something in her ear that made her smile. Bethany saw the smile and knew that nothing was wrong, so she went to her room and closed the door.

Her normal routine was to go to her room and finish any remaining homework. Then she would go into the attic until dinner.

She grabbed her diary and went into the attic. She noticed that some things had been moved but it wasn't a big deal to her. She understood that she shared the space in the attic with Amanda's family.  There was a small desk that Bethany wrote on in the corner of the attic by the window. Before she sat down at the desk, she saw an envelope had been placed on top of it. She was surprised. She looked around to see if Amanda was pulling a prank on her. No one ever invaded her space with anything like this before. The envelope was in eyes view but not arms reach. The name on the envelope was Ascetic Women's University and it was addressed to her. She froze like someone seeing a ghost for the first time. It was as if her shoes were nailed to the attics floor. She was two steps away from grabbing the very letter that would change the course of history. The strength was restored to her legs as she boldly stepped toward the desk to open the envelope. It was an acceptance letter from Ascetic Women's University. The University was offering her a full scholarship that included housing and everything. She screamed at the top of her lungs! Amanda and her mother heard her and ran to the attic. They opened the attic door and Bethany stood with the acceptance letter in her hand sobbing. Time stopped to her. Everything was magnified. Her ears recorded the sound of the creak of the hard wood floor as Amanda's mom rushed to comfort her. The embrace from her mom snatched her soul. She has never been comforted from a hug without intentions. What made that moment so memorable was that she felt something that she couldn't interpret, love.

## School life

Bethany made her choice; Ascetic Women's University was the school she saw a future at. Outside of majoring in Anthropology, she loved the principles and values the university stood on. The university took its name from the word Asceticism. Asceticism is a lifestyle characterized by abstinence from sensual pleasures. Because she has spent a lifetime of pleasure abstinence, she finally found a place that she felt a part of. Her emotions ran rapid during her campus visit. While the Admissions officer went over the information sessions, she marked up her brochure with all the things she wanted to do.

This was a new world for Bethany. Her first day was like a child visiting Disney World for the first time. Anxiety shadowed her and anticipation marked her steps. She finally connected with people that had the same mind, same interest and was headed in the same direction. She hit the ground running full speed. After being there for less than one semester, she already created a group with the deaf students at the university. She named the group Talking w/ Jaz, in honor of her sister. Talking w/Jaz (TWJ)was created as a social group that targeted improved interactions between the deaf and the hearing. What brought this issue to the light for her was during the campus visit. All the students had to listen to different speakers and watch videos about the school. None of the videos provided closed caption and they had Spanish interpreters but no one to interpret for the deaf.

There were twelve students that were deaf and one professor that spoke sign language at AWU. None of the deaf students took any courses with the professor that knew how to communicate with that community of students. After the group was established, Bethany thought it would be great to learn their language and to see if other students wanted to learn. The TWJ group posted flyers offering free sign language classes around the campus. They never imagined that so many teachers and students would be interested. Their group went from thirteen to one hundred and eighty. This group became one of the largest social groups at AWU. Her drive and determination created a lot of changes the first year she attended AWU. The university became proactive and included visual aids and strategies such as signing, fingerspelling, and lip-reading to help facilitate communication. The university even funded technology like assistive listening devices and real-time captioning, to help students access information and participate in class.

Bethany for the first time in her life has risen from the shadows and spun into leadership. Her leadership has echoed throughout the campus. The TWJ Group and other works that Bethany pioneered has landed on the desk of the Dean, Dr. Stanley Jacobs. I know that sound strange that there was a male dean in charge of a Women's University, but Dr. Stanley was a transgender. Before retiring and becoming the Dean of Ascetic Women's University (AWU), Stanley was a LGBT rights activist. His work was known around the world. He even fought the Board of Education to incorporate course studies like: Gender Identity, Gender Equality, and Trans fundamentals.

## The Meeting

Dr. Stanley set up a meeting with Bethany through administration. When she heard that the dean wanted to meet with her, she was gripped with fear.

"Why do he want to speak with me," she signed to her friends in the group.

They persuaded her to meet with him. They blindly encouraged her, not knowing how overwhelmed she had become. The closest she ever been to a man was the same person she blamed for her mom's death and for the misery her dad crowned Jazmine with. The thought of occupying the same space with a man was gut wrenching.

The day of the meeting, Bethany prepared herself by telling herself that she can do this. Her feet became weighted as she dragged them to the building where the dean waited. Dr. Stanley watched her dawdle at the entrance. He opened the door before her sweaty fist had a chance to knock.

"Come in Bethany, I been waiting on you. Come in and have a seat."

Bethany didn't speak nor did she make any eye contact with Stanley.

"It's a pleasure to finally meet you. I have heard so many wonderful things about you around campus," he said as an ice breaker.

Bethany's aura was so contentious that Dr. Stanley couldn't break through the barrier that her fear created. He stood in between her chair and his desk.

Leaning over, he softly said, "Bethany, look at me".

She raised her head and her face was filled with tears.

She clinched her fist, looked him in the eyes and yelled, "I fucking hate you!"

His secretary rushed in and asked was everything ok. He told her that everything was fine and to cancel the rest of his morning appointments.

Dr. Stanley immediately realized that her anger was deeper than this office visit. He sat in the chair next to Bethany.

"Why do you hate me?"

Bethany rage grew.

"I hate you because you killed my mom. Your selfishness destroyed our home and killed Jazmine. Why did you let momma die? You made me address Jazmine like she was my mom, she wasn't my mom, she was my sister!"

She became overcome with grief.

"It's your fault she killed herself, it's your fault I grew up without my mom's love. Can you imagine growing up and never feeling your mothers embrace? You should have just let me die instead. I HATE YOU!"

Bethany didn't realize how much pain she had buried in her heart. She was so angry that she didn't realize that she was standing over the doc with his shirt tightly clinched in her grasp. She collapsed to the floor, overcome with emotion. Dr. Stanley allowed her to have an uninterrupted release. This is what she needed. He assisted her back to her chair. After she had gotten herself composed, Dr. Stanley started the conversation over again. This time the angle was different.

"Bethany, I understand how painful things can be. Especially growing up with so much of your pain being rooted in animosity toward your dad. Now every masculine being resembles him. You are not the only one young lady. I don't know and it doesn't matter now what took place between you and your dad. You just had an emotional detonation that came from the inner most part of your soul, and you needed it."

Bethany jumped up from her chair and made her way toward the door.

"I'm so sorry! I never meant to disrespect you!"

Dr. Stanley stopped her and invited her to have a seat and began to console her and speak into her life.

"First of all, you didn't disrespect me. Sometimes men can be pieces of shit. Egotistical narcissist that uses their masculinity as a weight to hold women subjectively. They can destroy someone's life and live emotionless as if they have that human right".

Bethany laughed, "Oh, you think what I said was funny?"

"It's not what you said that was funny, it's just you are a man and you talking like that," she replied.

Stanley laughed as he went and sat behind his desk.

"I thought you were going to do your homework before you met me".

She grabbed a handful of tissue from his desk to wipe her face.

Dr. Stanley went on to say, "I am a transgender male."

"What," Bethany replied.

"Yes, born a woman and transitioned over twelve years ago. There is a part in my book where I explained that my transition had nothing to do with gender. My transition was from a broken vessel to a complete one. As a broken vessel I had no purpose. The reason any vessel is created is for use and what do you do with broken vessels? You throw them away. Instead of living my life in a dumpster ignored, useless and alone, I transitioned into the vessel I am now. My pen became my personality. After I started writing I finally developed the confidence to advocate for others like me in the LGBT community. The reason I gave you that moment to release was because I understand your agony. The man that called himself my dad took pleasure in creating trauma in my life. As young as I remembered I was not only my dad's sexual dump truck but also my uncles. I don't have much time to go into detail about how sick and cowardly they were, but you can read some of the stories in my book. Bethany, I carried pain everyday like a backpack filled with books. Most people allow those traumatic experiences to create unfillable voids in their life. I used that pain to become a better me. I made up in my mind that I would be a better man then my dad ever was."

Bethany asked, "Can I ask you a question?"

"Sure," he responded.

"Why me? Why did you want to meet with me, do you meet with all the girls that had messed up childhoods?"

"No. I met with you because I watched you move around this campus, creating groups and how well the students and professors respond to you. There is a light that illuminate your steps. I saw visions from the gods about you."

Bethany was blown away by his statement, "The gods!"

"Yes, the vision showed me that you will lead a revolution that would change the current world!"

Bethany starts to cry.

"Look at me, take your pain and trauma and use it as fuel to drive you into your destiny. This world will be different because of you. This is going to be very deep so I need your permission to share this with you, can I share this with you?"

She was nervous but she said yes.

"I haven't looked at your history or asked anyone about you, but the gods revealed something to me, and I feel I need to tell you. Your mom went as far as she could go in her research. She had to die for you to be birthed into your purpose. You will be remembered throughout generations Bethany."

She dropped her head and sobbed. Bethany left that meeting changed and so encouraged. It gave her a new outlook on life. During her third year in school, her sleep became troubled by dreams of her mom. This dream replayed several nights in a row. She heard some noise in the attic and slowly walked up the stairs. Bethany froze each night in the dream as she opened the door. It was her mom ravaging through her boxes. The last night she had the dream she asked her mom what she was looking for.

Her mom became panicked, "Where is the Treaty! You must find the Treaty!"

That was the last time she had that dream; she knew what had to be done. This is what started her search for the Treaty.

A concert was held at AWU, and it was sponsored by Talking w/Jaz. One of the group members named Janice was the interpreter for the growing deaf population at the university. One of the opening acts was a singer/activist named Constance. Bethany didn't know anything about any of the artist that performed that night. When she saw Constance perform that evening, she loved the sound of her charismatic singing. After the concert Constance slipped Bernice, a note requesting to meet with Bethany. When she gave her the note, Bethany didn't know how to respond. The note named a meeting place on campus shortly after the concert was over. She sat on a bench in front of the fountain. Constance came up from behind her and covered Bethany eyes with her hand.

" Guess who?"

"Umm, I am guessing that you are Constance," she replied.

"You are good, you guessed right on your first try. Let me formally introduce myself, I am Cindy Adams, but my fans call me Constance."

"So, should I call you Constance or Cindy?"

"I want you to be my friend not a fan so you can call me Cindy."

Cindy went on to tell her how she heard about her and wanted to be a part of her research on the location of the Treaty. They instantly became inseparable. She soon discovered that Cindy had been searching for the location of the Treaty for years. After a lengthy conversation, Bethany learned that the 911 attack on the Pentagon used a plane as a deflection from the truth.

The truth was that Cindy's dad lead a team of ex-military men/women to breach the pentagon to recover the Treaty on September 11, 2001. Her dad's name was Russel Paige, but you will never find his name in any news archives. The government wiped his name from existence after the breach. Since the Pentagon was called the Department of Defense, the only way to get in was to infiltrate its defenses. That's exactly what he done.

The Pentagon was fortified. The shape of its construction and wall system alone were structured to handle missile attacks and survive. If it was compared to a military vehicle, it would be a tank. The very fabric of this place was impenetrable. After years of research Mr. Paige finalized the way he would take the Pentagon and recover the Treaty. History proved that cyber-attacks would neutralize their security systems long enough for him and his team to gain access to The Vault. The morning of the attack, he had one of his team members that worked with the computer systems to sound the alarm for a cyber hack. The protocol was faulty. During cyber-attacks, every door and secured area switched to manual lockdown. If not, the hacker would have access to every department since everything was ran by the online computer system. Five members of his team were responsible for the lockdown of the floors below ground level. They planned, during the lockdown, to leave those areas unlocked so those that would seize The Vault would have access.

Before the staged cyber-attack, he stored bombs and extra weapons in several marked closets around the Pentagon. Each bomb had to be detonated by a code sent from his phone. The only problem with that was all phone access and signals were cut off in case of cyber-attack. The cameras also go silent to control the perpetrators access. He decided to chance it.

Everything was smooth at first and went as planned. His team made it as far as the first underground floor. Federal agents were notified by radio that there was a breach. No one ever found out who notified them. All sixteen members of his team were shot and killed. When they discovered that the cyber-attack was a smokescreen for a domestic attack, the system was armed again. Mr. Paige saw that the cameras and security doors had been activated. He was then able to use his phone to detonate the bombs on the west side of the Pentagon. Before he was able to detonate any more, he also was shot by federal agents. He survived his injuries and was taken to a secret location. The damage from the bombs was so horrific, it looked like a foreign attack on American soil. That is also the way the picture was painted. The history books tell their story of what happened on that day and it was never written how close Mr. Paige and his team were to uncovering the location of the Treaty.

There were no medical records to prove that any of them had been shot or injured. Conspiracy theorists believe he wasn't taken to the hospital at all but to a place in the Pentagon, interrogated and killed. According to Cindy's testimony, the government raided his home, business, and the place where his team met. All those locations were burned. It was rumored that his wife and two sons died in a house fire the same day of the attack.

Bethany was blown away by her story.

She asked Cindy, "If the government killed Mr. Paige family, why are you still alive?"

She explained to her that her dads name wasn't put on her birth certificate. She carried her mother's maiden name, Adams. Even though he had a new wife and family, Cindy's mom continued to have a relationship and work close with Mr. Paige up until his death.

## Gained Access

Bethany has grown to be a focused activist that found pleasure in research and discovery. She is in her third year toward getting her Doctorate Degree. Cindy is following her father's brain rhythms by establishing a team of revolutionaries to finish what her dad started. She slowly infiltrated the pentagon by following the blueprint her dad left. She wasn't just an artist but was gifted when it came to technology. In 2018, the government released to the public that a foreign entity cyber-hacked the Pentagon. They even gave him an identity. This was another cover up. Cindy hacked into the system to see if the security had been updated or were they challenged with the old system. She was right, the procedures were outdated, everything went to manual lockdown. She was confident that her plan would work especially against the same system her dad exposed. There was always a conspiracy that her dad had a mole, planted by the government that caused his demise.

Now everyone was in place. Cindy had over thirty women placed throughout the Pentagon. Several of Bethany's friends from the Talking w/Jaz group and other groups she formed have joined her in her endeavors. People gravitated to Bethany. She was a born leader and those that followed her and heard her story were inspired. Their dreams can finally come true. They both dreamed of a day where they could make their parents proud.

Finally, the time has come. During the Presidential Elections in 2020, depending on the outcome, they planned on cyber hacking the security and retrieving the Treaty. Bethany used the campus of AWU as headquarters for their meetings so it would go unnoticed. She was never questioned. Dr. Stanley gave her access to whatever she needed. He even used money from the programs she created at the university to fund her efforts.

**The Vault**

The President wasn't reelected. This was a perfect time to create a nationwide diversion. Bethany, along with her team and other supporters created small cells around D.C. They began protesting the election results. Their voice grew louder as spooled untruths about the electoral votes from each state arose. They even created claims saying the ballots were stolen by the opposite party. When that built enough momentum, she used it as a snowball effect to attack the Capital.

Her plan worked, she had thousands of men and women ready to fight against what they felt was injustice. In less than one week, the Capital take over was underway. Emotions were high. The United States of America has become the Divided States of America. The nation was facing a domestic uprising. Because of this, the government cleared the Pentagon and sent most of their armed guards and troops to the Capital for fear that thousands of insurgents would overtake it. The barricades outlined the Capital like a blueprint. Scaffolded walls were built to keep these protestors from breaching. Bethany worked her way to the side of the capital and broke out a window. The sound of broken glass echoed across the steps of the Capital. At that moment, the protestors became terrorists and attacked the Capital. This riot was uncontrollable.

Cindy along with other staff at the Pentagon watched in awe. Its time. She took out her laptop and cyber-hacked the system from within. The Pentagon went into manual lockdown. All the cameras went offline and the phones. One thing that Cindy did different from her dad was that she didn't plant any bombs or bring any weapons. She felt that being militant is what got her dad killed. After leaving the doors unlocked and the lack of staff, she simply walked to The Vault undetected. She met four female agents that was a part of her team, they opened the door. She couldn't believe that she made it that far. Even though she was confident in the plan, it was mythical watching it come to fruition. She looked around as if it was a set up. It seemed too easy, almost eerie. She was overcome with chills as she grabbed the heavy stack of documents that made up the Treaty.

Her friends voice echoed throughout the Vault.

"Let's go!"

Cindy came to herself and made hast to leave. She placed the Treaty in a carrying case and made her way to her department. All the doors were locked, the area was secured. It was like her, and her team just exited a dream. All you could hear was footsteps on the silent corridors. Bethany and those that followed her made their way back to the hotel they were staying in. She was a nervous wreck. She couldn't contact Cindy until the lockdown was lifted. It seemed like hours.

**The Hotel Room**

The lockdown was lifted. All the cameras were back on, and the systems were up and operating. The Nation's attention was on the uprising at the Capital. All government buildings have been shut down by the President. This was Cindy's way out. As soon as her department head announced the shutdown, she grabbed her things, along with the Treaty and left. She ran to her car never looking back.

The news of the riots at the Capital were live across the world and Bethany haven't heard any news on the Treaty. Suddenly, there is a panicked knock at the hotel room door. Everyone in the room froze with fear. Bethany slowly walked to the door. Before she could look through the peep hole.

Cindy said, "Open the door Bethany, I got it!"

This is the moment they have been waiting for. Cindy sat the Treaty on the bed, and they embraced each other and cried.

Bethany then took out her phone and began to scan each document. She was in shock. An unamended Treaty that has only been seen by our forefathers. There was over fifty pages. The signatures of this country's forefathers were priceless. It took her over two hours to scan the Treaty. The pages were well preserved, but she still handled them graciously. Bethany put them back in its' carrying case and handed it over to Cindy. She agreed to store the documents in a secured place. No one was to know this location but her and Cindy. They embraced each other. The hotel room became a sanctuary of tears. Everyone was choked up. It was so surreal that everyone signed goodbye and I love you because they were muted by admiration.

She sent the scanned copies to herself, Cindy and a third person. Each computer and phone that they communicated with was instantly destroyed. They transferred the Treaty through a ghost filing system. That way it made it untraceable. Their plan was for Bethany to go back to school and for everyone to return to their jobs at the Pentagon. There was no contact made between the two overnight. Cindy believed that the phones were tapped so they agreed to talk on burner (untraceable) phones the next day.

**Next morning**

Bethany was exhausted. She spent all night reading through the pages of the Treaty. She was awaked by an alarming dream. This dream was different from the ones that she had before. Bethany dreamed that she was in the attic writing in her diary. She heard someone burst through the attic door.

It was her mom yelling, "Wake up and get out!"

She jumped from the bed. Before she was able to grab any of her things, federal agents kicked in the door. Her face was immediately covered with a blackening cloth and her hands zip tied. It is believed that they took her to a secluded place at the Pentagon. It was also rumored that she was held in a room along with Cindy and the rest of her team except for one member. Bethany and Cindy and everyone that participated in the attack on the Pentagon were never heard from again. Her best friend from the town of Hawley was found dead along with her mother. It was reported that they died together in a house fire.

Dr. Stanley heard the news and was devastated. The university just lost a young pioneer. They were reported lost after the riots but those that were close to them knew what happened.

## Exposed

It took Dr. Stanley Grumple several months to process what happened to Bethany. The truth of the events at the Pentagon became another government cover up. All the things Bethany done at AWU and away from the university was noticed on a large scale. Dr. Stanley honored Bethany by awarding her with an Honorary Doctorate Degree. It only took three months before a statue was erected of her in the courtyard of AWU where she first met Cindy. Bethany knew that she could trust Stanley. That's why she sent him the extra copies of the Treaty. Only Cindy and Bethany knew the plan was to give the Dean a copy just in case something happened to them. Dr. Stanley was always known for being a fearless activist, but this hit him differently. He stepped away from his seat as Dean to concentrate on fulfilling Bethany's dream of exposing the truth of our forefather's suppression. She set the bar very high. Even though she was young, she made every step count. Dr. Stanley, being motivated by her efforts, got the courage to release the scanned copies of the Treaty. He understood that this could cost him his life also.

He took that copy and went public with this information. If he stayed in the public's view, he felt he was safe. He had to move stealth like. If the government found that the files were leaked, they would mop him up and everyone he connected too. The first thing he did was to go live in a secluded place via social media. He already had a large following, especially from the LGBTQ community. When he spoke, people listened. That's why he favored Bethany because she always magnetized her audience.

Dr. Stanley had multiple cameras set up that connected to different live feeds. He knew he had to expose as much as he could before the government shut down the feed. After his countdown began, he had to accept the fact that he would have to remain underground until he is not spooked by his shadow. He went live! The internet went silent as he spoke first about what happened to the two young ladies. Social media blew up. Everyone was sharing the live on their individual pages. He started reading different parts of the first signed page of the Treaty:

*'In the beginning God conceived man. Man is the only part of His creation that mirrored the Creator. The ability to produce life is in his choosing and rest in the loins of the nature of man. With sovereignty man shall rule the fem of his pleasure. The fem was formed as eye delight for the man. When she is selected, by force or free-will she then will be called female. That will indicate that she has been conquered. An unselected fem shall be left independently in her shame. Ascendancy will be concealed by way of protection. The man shall labor and war with his hands and rule his house with the strength of his heel. The integrity of his household is honored by his rule. His home is constructed by subservience.*

*A female's beauty rest solely in obeying he that made her female. A fem is subjected to her father's servitude, she can only be released if she is conquered. If the female rebel from her covering and chose not to obey she shall be imprisoned.'*

He skipped around some of the articles. He felt the need to expose the religious section, so he read some of the pages in the Treaty about religious suppression. Several times he had to pause because he became emotional as the truth was being read. Religion was weaponized to keep women submerged in oppression. The live feeds were up long enough to rattle the cages of world known feminist and other women's rights organizations. Churches, synagogues, and Mosques became inflamed with anger. Many Muslim women rebelled by burning their hijabs and taken up arms. They were willing to die for this new freedom. The more the government and world leaders tried to silence the released Treaty pages, the more it spread. He did enough to stir the pot but not enough to bring things to its boiling point.

Dr. Stanley live feed had thousands of onlookers around the world. All the major news stations are going crazy. Finally, someone has debunked the myth of the Treaty. This has become a historic moment. News of the Treaty was spreading faster than the Bubonic Plague. The President declared a national emergency to block the airways. The federal government was searching for a signal to his location, but Cindy set up this bunker and made sure it was untraceable. The President directed Americans to focus on the horrific crimes that took place months ago at the Capital. He quickly talked about those that were killed and injured during the attack to manipulate the people psychologically. The main reason was to make the news of the Treaty look like fake news. Dr. Stanley was now cast as an extremist that cyber-hacked the broadcasting system and spreading false propaganda.

"There is no Treaty hidden in the Pentagon," the President reported.

He also said," Anyone that is caught spreading lies against this country will be considered terrorist and will be dealt with to the fullest extent of the law!"

News outlets all around the world began to repeat his rhetoric. Somehow, Stanley live feeds were cut and all his social media accounts frozen. His face and Ascetic Women's University was plastered across every television station. The university fired him immediately to save the school. They released a statement informing the public that they are not responsible, nor do they support any of his actions. Dr. Stanley was forced to stay underground. The sad part about it all was that he put his life in jeopardy to never be heard from again.

## Aftermath

It has been over a year of fighting. Men in government, business owners, husbands, and religious leaders wasn't letting this news chip away at the foundation of this country and this world. They viewed this as the destruction of civilization. Women angrily protested all around the world as men repeated that the Treaty was a hoax and fake news.

Several groups of women around the nation formed armed militias in this short span of time. They were called the Web. The Web was formed by an ex-military sergeant. No one knew her government name. She was always known as Recluse. She and her follows believed in blood for blood. They were overcome with a hatred for the man. This hatred grew like cancer. It spread to the most stable homes. Couples that had been married for years found themselves in divorce. These riots and protest from women's rights groups and Web, push for women power and freedom began to lose steam. The repeated broadcasting that dispelled the Treaty's validity caused many women to lose heart and go back to a lifestyle of suppression, but things were never the same.

## New President

The President that was elected before the Treaty were exposed, was the first in history to select a woman as Vice President. America was blinded by gender. When she became Vice President, most of the organizations that fought diligently for equality became silenced by complacency. Many women felt their goals were reached and change has come. There remained a select vestige that knew that the Treaty was real and needed to be exposed to the world to have true liberation. No one imagined what took place two years after that, the President died in office. The Vice President is now the first woman to sit in this seat of power. It was rumored that she had her hand in his demise, it wasn't substantiated. One thing for sure, she did her homework and understood that the president was given power by the U.S Constitution over treaties. She immediately made an executive order to release the pages of the Treaty after her inauguration. The senate fought her decision knowing the detriment it would have on the current world.  The release of the Treaty will cause women to think for themselves and not through the eye of men nor religion.  Over two thirds of the senate were women, they took up a resolution of ratification. With their consent the President retrieved the Treaty and released it to the public.

The news of this was bigger than Armstrong's walk on the moon. This was the push women needed to break from the cocoon of suppression. Her decision and power sparked a chain reaction across the globe. There was no more denying the truth. Women rose.

Educators dismantled the Treaty page by page, article by article. They fought the board of education and had all books that followed the principles of the Treaty deleted. Television shows, music and movies that spoke the same language as the Treaty were banned forever. Religious leaders, men, and women alike, began to denounce centuries of teachings.

Teaching from the Bible, 'Women should not have authority over a man, women are the weaker vessels, origin was questioned.'

All around the world women revolted against those sacred artifacts. Some female radicals burned their holy books. The Web grew. Recluse led these woman-like soldiers. Their entire mission was to crucify religion and never give it time to resurrect.

Churches and places of worship that held on to tradition, were destroyed and some even burned by the Web. The President called traditional religious teachings, sacrilegious doctrine which was deemed hate speech. After her second term in office, she had it written into law through an Executive Order, any violations were punishable up to time in prison. The church went underground along with other religions that wasn't wholly abandoned. This was the first time in history that all religions formed an alliance called the Remnant. The Remnant put aside the racial divide and even the ages of religious division and became unified.

This unification formed a one world religion. Some of these sects of the Remnant gathered arms to defend themselves against Web. There were even women that held to the traditional foundation that they were religiously rooted in and served their husbands. The Remnant did separate and denounce the agreement made with a Western New Guinea group known as the Flesh feeders. They fled Indonesia and hid amongst the Remnant. The Elders soon found out that they practiced cannibalism after an attack on one of the compounds. Most of the dead were either burned or buried. The Flesh feeders were banned all around the old world and even in the new, because they ate them.

Before the news of the Treaty, women were 80% of the parishioners of organized religion. Now women made up less than a tithe of the underground Remnant. The small religious sects that went underground was 90% men. Men turned to God like never before. They didn't know what to do. Most of their women left them. Suicide rates for males were through the roof and God was the only answer to this new equation called life.

The President was elected for a third term. This was possible because she succeeded the president after his death in office. United States never had another male president after her. She proved to be more than an advocate for women. She faced off with world leaders, male and female alike. She was likened to a dragon. Those that opposed her were consumed by her voice. Because of her fierceness in leadership, women followed the path she burned before them. Women strategically became rooted in every branch of government. Decisions, laws, and government was solely in the hands of women. The Treaty caused them to become insistently proactive instead of reactive.

The men on the other hand withdrew from positions of power. Without the woman, men became ineffectual. For centuries, women were the backbone of men. Now that their crutch was removed, men collapsed to paralysis. During that time, they became like infants in learning to do everything on their own. Men were not clueless to everyday living. Cooking and cleaning was as natural to man as grooming and hunting. It was the realization of it all that broke their spirits. The Treaty gave men a damnable sense of authority and power. They realized their egotistical forefathers plotted against their own women. Men's headship came from suppression of what they thought was a weaker vessel. Many of the men began to doubt themselves and question their existence.

Women were enlightened. Affirmative Action ushered so many women to their seats. Some wasn't qualified for the positions they received but companies hired them anyway. The momentum the Treaty caused was now unstoppable. Determined and angry, women were full steam ahead. Thirteen years after the release of the Treaty, the US and other countries passed a Reparations Act of 2033. Women of different races gained reparations for centuries of oppression, forced servitude, and suppression by way of religion and education. With those reparations, many started investing into other women ran companies and science institutes. Racism was silenced. There wasn't any tension or dissension between the races. One thing man took pride in, was building infostructures but women were known for building each other.

Years of fighting for equality, women knew they still wasn't equal to men. Men were biologically stronger, more industrial, ingenuitive and solution oriented. Women used their whit to invest in factories that created women friendly machinery. To maintain infrastructure and a healthy environment, a trash system was in place to get rid of waste/trash. This was a job that most women would pass up even with equal hiring opportunities. So, women invested in companies that made the jobs easier for females. The more money they invested, the more machines created to take the place of what was considered, men's work. No more dumping trash cans with your hands, every city had trash trucks with motorized arms. Once this system was in place everywhere, women took over those jobs too.

It took another five years to make the workforce into work from home jobs. Women were more prone to at home jobs and even jobs that required talking on the phone. Office employment became a thing of the past. Most companies saved on overhead by allowing employees to work from home. Shopping online wasn't an option anymore; it was the only way to shop. Grocery stores were delivery by drone/worker only. Major auto manufacturers created all machine assembly lines. Security companies thought they would profit from upgrades and more monitored security systems. These systems ended up replacing the security that women naturally found in men.

A special force was created to monitor homes with this system called Oxicure. Oxicure used a system that not only video monitored their customers but was the first security company to use audio surveillance. New privacy acts allowed for audio and video monitoring. Each home or business that were monitored by Oxicure had their own security fingerprint. This allowed the customer access to personalize their systems. The systems were called identITy (IT). IT was given a name and learned when to enter conversations, raise concerns about health, alert family in case of emergencies and was able to lock and unlock everything for security purposes. These systems advanced more after the Virus. Oxicure policed homes and businesses better than the police dept. They had the authority to send out patrol vehicles if they saw anything that looked suspicious.

The need, for what man had to offer dwindled. The adult industry created everything a woman needed for sexual satisfaction and pleasure. Men never fathomed that women used them to create a system to get rid of themselves. The work industry was secured and able to be maintained by women. Trades like electricians, engineers, carpenters, and plumbers still lacked the female presence. Programs were created to increase salaries in those fields to motivate women. It worked.

**Virus**

There was a company created that was established in the early 2000's called Fertili-com. Fertili-com (FC) was created as a fertility clinic and couples counseling facility. They counseled couples that had issues with childbirth and other family related issues.

Abortion was on the rise, so FC struggled to stay afloat. That present world focused more on a woman's choice to terminate a birth than a woman's desire to give birth. Abortion was trending. FC was faced with a decision. To avoid shutting down, they agreed to a buyout by an undisclosed sister company of Planned Parenthood. They kept the name and even some of the services. The new owners were funded by some of the world's largest feminist and woman focused organizations. FC added labs, hired scientist, not to cure cancer but to find ways to procreate without men.

The stock in this company grew years before the Treaty was released. Money was being dumped into FC for research. All these years of testing and artificial insemination, it was known that for fertilization, sperm and an egg was needed. There was no way of escaping that natural fact. Their practice was Vitro Fertilization (IVF). The process by which an egg is injected with sperm in a laboratory dish for fertilization to occur outside of the body. This type of testing has been ongoing for years at FC.

Scientist there created a wombless incubator system called Lab-womb (Lamb). A Lamb is an artificial womb that was created to carry a fetus full term without a female host. Limitations were presented in earlier years with the Lamb but after technology advancements, Lamb made it possible to choose eye color, hair type, race and even sex of the child. Childbirth became a catalog of choices. The Lamb made this possible. While the world was in turmoil, FC made a discovery.

**Old Way**

Normal childbirth consists of either X or Y chromosomes. If a sperm with an X chromosome fertilize an egg the resulting zygote will be female XX. If the sperm which fertilizes the egg have a Y chromosome, the zygote will be male XY. Scientist discovered through the Lamb that the Y chromosome could be removed, resulting in only XX childbirths. The scientist that discovered this breakthrough name was Dr. Zia Moore. Before you learn about her discovery, let me tell you what I discovered about Zia before she became Dr. Moore.

Zia Moore was conceived as a product of date rape in a small town in Ohio. Her mom, whose name was Xavier, was a three-year science major that studied Biology. Xavier dreams were to become a Scientist at all costs. She struggled with her lab work and asked the professor for help. He told her that he had an event to attend away from the school and told her if she goes, he is willing to help. She agreed. He didn't tell her that the event was a dinner/swinger's party. A lot of the professors at the university was a part of a secret society. They were into sex parties. Little did she know, she was the dessert for the night. After the night was digested, the professor dropped her off. The next morning, she had no memory of the evening before. Due to embarrassment, that night was locked away as a foggy memory.

Abortion wasn't an option because her mom was 22 weeks pregnant when she found out. She felt forced to carry her. Zia felt that her mom was forced to love her. Every day was a constant reminder from her mom about how she was conceived. Zia never met the sperm donors, but she grew to hate him and herself for the way she was conceived. She hated the idea of a woman not having control of their own body. The Treaty gave her a new sense of empowerment. She was unable to form a loving relationship with her mom.

Zia was broken, abused, disowned, and ignored. She used that as motivation to be what she always wanted to be, a scientist. Now to fast forward, Zia Moore graduated at the top of her class. She was always fascinated with DNA, reproduction, and sperm analysis. Her focus was microscopic when it came to detail. When it came to a social life, it was nonexistent. The lab and all her work was her life source.

FC did a 3-year trial run, led by Dr. Moore, in 2026 and it was successful. Through the Lamb and artificial insemination, only XX chromosomes were produced. After the Reformation Act of 2033 her discovery was funded on a larger scale. Sponsors wanted to eradicate the Y chromosome from existence. Dr. Moore continued her research into the matter.

Unemployment

Men led in unemployment for the first time since World War II. Women took over the workforce. It was part two of the Women's Liberation Movement. Men that weren't in the medical field and engineering struggled to find work. Fertili-Com capitalized on their struggle by opening over 7,000 sperm clinics around the US alone. These clinics were paid sperm banks. FC Clinics allowed men to donate sperm up to four times a week. Thousands of men came weekly. The overflow was so great that the US teamed with other countries and opened these types of clinics worldwide. Men never questioned why so many sperm banks were opening. Since jobs were so scarce, many men just saw it as a paycheck. Women disassembled religion, took over the workforce, created machinery and AI's to replace the strength that men had to offer for generations. Dr. Zia Moore discovered a way to exist without the Y.

By 2040, the sperm banks and storge facilities were filled. They had enough sperm to repopulate the earth if need be. All the sperm collected was cleaned of all Y chromosomes. During Dr. Moore years of research, she learned that the X chromosome alone exist without defect, sickness, and disease. The three-year experiment back in 2026 resulted in health. There were no autism births, blindness nor deaf children. To procreate a XY was needed to determine the sex of a child. Feminist felt that men still had power over gender, in some ways it was true. It was the combination of the sperm and egg that created these childbirth defects and diseases. She didn't find the cure for disease, but she discovered the reason for it. Centuries of knowledge has been silenced. They learned how to extract the Y from the sperm and produce a generation of Fem babies. Dr. Zia also discovered the weakness that men carried. It existed all along in their DNA.

To weaken the male, the Y chromosome must be attacked. Without the Y, women call live in purity and without sickness. She conducted a trial experiment. Men were paid for this trial and asked no questions because of the scarcity off jobs. After all disclosures were signed, she had over 100 test beds. The Lamb proved that XX chromosomes can exist without the Y but the next challenge was seeing if the host of the Y could survive without the X.

This trial was to eradicate the Y from the host and see the affects. It was called Cell Lessening. She created a vaccine aimed to attack the Y chromosome to prove her hypothesis. The extraction of the Y from the host's DNA proved to be clinically successful but detrimental to those that partook of the trial. The first tester that the trial proved fatal, only took three weeks. It was reported that all the volunteers suffered migraine headaches two days after receiving the shot. The other symptoms were like a common cold that lasts for about two weeks. Three weeks in and most of the men seemed just fine. Suddenly they all started to feel like their bodies were on fire. Some of the lab attendants said that it smelt like cooking flesh. Over 80% of the men developed fluctuated fevers. The highest was 116 degrees and the lowest was 70 degrees. After five weeks, all the testers died. There was no way for the host to survive without the Y together with the X.

Dr. Zia next step was to emit this virus somehow through the air. Her researchers suggested using mosquitoes like the Big Buzz Experiment in the 1950s. The government tested yellow fever on modest black populated communities by using mosquitoes as host. This method proved to be harmfully effective. Thousands of people were infected with yellow fever.

With this information, the lab injected thousands of mosquitos with the virus that Dr. Zia created. Fertili-Com used their connection with the US government and was able to use special military planes to drop the host. She released them over a small town in Tennessee. It only took three days after the first round of mosquitos were dropped before the news media began to flood the stations with this new virus that only affected males. They called it Chromovirus (CV). They used over 400,000 infected hosts. In less than a span of a week, the numbers of the infected rose to over 6000 Y chromosome carriers. As far as three counties from the original drop, another 2000 were affected with CV. The hospitals haven't seen anything like this. There was no treatment. One thing that Dr. Zia never figured into the equation was how this virus would affect animals. The virus was carried to animals, and they died within days of infection. The people's outrage over the animals dying was louder than the cry for the man and boys that succumb to CV. Over a months' time, the numbers began to grow slowly around the country.

Fertilicom took the virus and sold it to researchers in other countries. Dr. Zia was upset. She went to the owners of Fertilicom about this violation of her work and research. They dismissed her and informed her that all her research belonged to Fertilicom. Security removed her without allowing her to retrieve any of her belongings. Like most Americans, she brought her work home. She stored a lot of data on secret files. Since she created the virus, she also had a vaccine for the virus.

A scientist in Russia purchased the virus and developed a host cell in the respiratory tract that would make this virus airborne. A trial release of this strain was deadly and spread a lot faster than CV. This strain was called CV11. It swept through countries like Influenza. Once this strain was discovered in California, the World Health Organization (WHO) stepped in and declared CV11 a pandemic. The rate of Y Chromo deaths happened faster than graves could be dug. Reports say mass graves were dug and mankind and animals were buried together. Their names were engraved on a memorial wall.

 The world was in shock. Women were burying their sons and daughters were burying their fathers. Men fought back through isolation, mask, social distancing but none of that helped.  It has only been a year since Dr. Zia released CV and its now a worldwide pandemic. The source was unknown to the public and no cure was available. The president used her executive powers and ordered a shut down. This shut down took place all around the world. During the shutdown the government used the US Census as a key to assess the homes of civilians. They were looking for a way to administer a monitoring device in men. This would also expose those underground entities like the church.

## Exile

When the Y chromos were expurgated. They were immediately treated with a pill designed by Fertili-Com. This capsule contained a tracking device that reported to the administering team when it was digested. Men were convinced that the pill was for their betterment, it was only aspirin. CV11 worked slower than the original bloodborne strain but the airborne strain was more contagious. To protect the female population, men and boys were exiled. Women had to protect themselves and this is the only way they saw fit. Y chromosomes were forced to stay outside each city. Men were only allowed in with permit to remove dead animals and mankind from the streets. They wore special hazmat suits to protect the public from CV11.

The WHO approved a vaccine created by Fertili-Com and the new president mandated the vaccine to every biological male. The vaccine was administered at the city gates. The vaccine that was given was nothing more than Chromovirus that Dr. Zia Moore created. It took only a year in a half before the virus cleansed itself of everything that possessed the Y chromosome.

## Reconstruction

2042 was called the Year of Grief. Most of the men died outside of the city with no comfort, no funeral, and no closure. Some women felt that the government's (Orders) plan was to have a man-less society. The idea of women running the world was just a fantasy. After the Year of Grief, it was reality.

It's time for reconstruction. As some still grieved and graves were freshly covered, the leaders of the present world destroyed all movies, music, books, pictures, and images of mankind. It was easy to do because everything was stored digitally. Phones and computers were wiped clean with one update. Just with a click of a button, those memories were gone. Wiped from history. The main issue that the new world faced was the memory of mankind.

The government worked closely with Virtual Reality (VR) creators. Mind altering games had been on the market since the early 2000's. These games were marketed for children as an experiment to see the complexity of mind alterations. The government monitored the VR and used it in crime data. The more shooting games that were sold to a certain geographic, shootings and crime grew in that area as a result. The VR stimulated the part of the brain that separated reality from fiction. Now it's time to use this technology on the survivors of the old world. With this cleanse, they were able to pinpoint the part of the brain that stored past memory. For the new world to flow in unity, fems needed a clean canvas. All fems over the age of 6 had to go through the three stages of Mind Cleanse. This process was painless but affective. This was a worldwide mandate. Once the three stages were finished, they received a stamp of completion. This stamp was a microchip placed in the palm of their hands. If they didn't have the stamp, they weren't allowed to buy food, sell, or trade anything. Even employment was denied to those without the stamp.

It took over six months to get everyone cleansed. Most of the women that were part of the Remnant refused the cleanse. They claimed it was the Mark of the Beast. The Web also refused. Those that refused became residents in the Outwards.

# 1

The year is 2063. For centuries females (fems) were told that they needed mankind to exist. It has been over 20 years since the last known male died. In Femdom there isn't even a memory of mankind. In this New World, it looks like fems are doing good on their own.

Courtney lives in the City of New Daphne with her parent Janice. To maintain the buildings and communities, those that received the stamp moved inward bound (Inwards) towards downtown. Most of the buildings were converted into housing, since so many corporations converted to remote jobs. Condensing the living to the downtown sections of each city made maintaining easier. Those fems that refused to get the mental cleanse were sent to the Outwards. Along with convicted felons, the Orders put them out of the city gates. The Outwards did not have any access to stores, police protection nor security. They were considered a threat to Femdom and were treated as outcasts. Their memory has become an enemy to Femdom. Without the mental cleanse they still remembered the days that are Undiscussed by law. Violators discovered discussing the old world were arrested. Over time the Outwards minds grew cloudier of the past and their children only remembered what they were told. Traumatic experiences normally find a safe place to hide in the brain. In their case, their hearts grew cold, and the key to it was lost forever.

It became customary in Femdom that fems left home either for union or they are over the age of 21. Courtney is 22 but didn't want to leave her parent alone. The real reason she haven't left home is she doesn't want to be alone. Courtney was an introverted loner with one true friend name Lacey. Since she was a young fem, she felt she wasn't understood. Anxious, yes, an overthinker, yes, accepted by others, no.

Her parent Janice was also a loner. A lot of fems her age had to get a brain cleansing to receive the stamp that allowed them access to the Inwards. She was filled with Old World wisdom but blended in to avoid persecution and prosecution. She humbly worked at one of the housing buildings downtown as a housekeeper. Courtney had no memory of the old world, but she believed that she was hunted by a monster from there. She was troubled by the same dream for some time now. She asked Janice for advice on overcoming bad dreams.

"Always drink a cup of water before you go to bed, that will help you clear your mind and balance your hormones. I also learned not to eat anything three hours before bedtime and cut the projector view (PV) off. How do you expect to sleep good, watching that junk like Teen Love?"

"Wait, hold up, Teen Love is a good show. I'm on the 8th episode. Did you know Shelley and Crystal saved enough money to pick out a baby!"

"See that's the junk I'm talking about. Why would two teens even be thinking about having a baby? First of all, they don't work, they are still in transitional education, and they would have to have at least $25,000 before they can even knock on the door of Fertilicom. Stop watching all that junk and your dreams would probably be more productive."

Courtney didn't agree with her about the show, but she did take all the other things she said into consideration.

That night, as Courtney prepared for bed, she took a shower, brushed her teeth, and checked her messages against the mirror in her restroom. Oh, I forgot to tell you, phones were no longer handheld devices. In the world of Femdom, they used Projected Technology. This technology was an insert just below the skin of either your right or left palm. You could touch any glass surface and it would project your phones screen. After letting her phone sleep, she grabbed a cup of water, and drank it. She even cut the

PV off. This night she hoped would be different. A peaceful night sleep with no nightmares, she was wrong.

The dream reoccurred. Somehow, Courtney took a wrong turn and found herself outside the city walls with the Outwards. The Outwards were poor and lawless. The children looked feeble and hungry. One of the children in the dream was holding what looked like her younger sibling. As Courtney got closer, she was able to notice the young fem ribs through the small unwashed t-shirt that hung off her shoulders. Courtney pitied her. She kneeled next to her and pulled a piece of bread from her pocket. She was suddenly surrounded by children of all ages. They lifted her against her will as she struggled to get loose.

  She screamed, "Put me down, put me down!"

Her screams went unheard. The night became silenced. All anyone could hear was Courtney's voice bouncing off the walls and echoing through the streets as she was exalted. She was placed by a monument in the center of a park. She was scared to even look at the monument. Her breathing became asthmatic. When she looked around, she was left alone. The sound of a rusty chain from a swing was heard as it swung back and forward with no operator. A chill laced darkness overcame her. Courtney ran and hid behind the monument. Peeking from behind it, she was gripped with fear. A tall shadowy figure stood on the other side of the park. The moons glare was blocked by its shoulder's width. This monster had leather for skin. She never seen anything like it before. The shoulders were two times the size of a fems. Its face was covered with hair and the hands were large like a bear's paw. It stood on two legs as it walked. She put her back against the monument and heard what sounded like thunder from its mouth, "Courtney!" She woke up frightened and in a deep sweat. Brandy, her security identITy, responded to her heart rate.

"Courtney, are you ok? Your heart rate is racing, and your body temperature is rising. Do you need medical attention?"

She is trying to catch her breath. These dreams feel so real. She sat up on the end of the bed.

"No, I don't need medical attention. It was just another damn nightmare."

She looked at the cup of water next to her bed and shook her head.

"Oh, drink some water, that will cleanse your mind", she said sarcastically. "Damn my parent, water is not the answer for everything!"

She places her pillow over her face and screams in it.

"I could have watched my show if I knew I would still have the same nightmare!"

Brandy is being petty this morning. Courtney will soon start to believe that she has a mind of her own.

"Do you want me to wake Janice and repeat what you said?"

"No Brandy, with your telling ass. If I wanted to tell Janice that I would just say it to her face. I can't even talk to myself around you. You always want to repeat something. Do you ever turn off, go to sleep, or to work, damn!"

"My job is to make sure you are secure, and I am programmed to never sleep. How can I keep an eye on you if they were created to close."

Courtney was upset that her sleep continues to be disrupted by this dream. She is starting to have the same dream three to four times a week.

"What time is it Brandy?"

"The time is 5:45am."

She jumped up from the bed. Her alarm is normally set for 5am.

"Why didn't you wake me? I need to get a system upgrade. I probably change your identITy to Stacy or something."

She is panicking, she hate been late for work. Courtney is scrambling around looking for her uniform.

"I attempted to wake you several times. I played your favored song, Desire. I rang freedom bells for 5 minutes at full volume and you continued to sleep. You were unaware because you were in REM sleep. The Outwards were carrying you to the monument."

Courtney froze. "Brandy, repeat everything you just said."

"I attempted to wake you several times. I played your favored song, Desire. I rang freedom bells for 5 minutes at full volume and you continued to sleep. You are unaware because you were in REM sleep. The Outwards were carrying you to the monument."

She sat on the bed and laced up her shoes.

"How the fuck do you know what I dreamed? Do you know what I'm thinking about?"

"I do not know what you are thinking. I only knew what the dream was about because you told your parent about your visions. Your brain rhythms and heart rate point out the parts of your dream like a map."

Courtney was okay with the answer, but she felt that Brandy knowing her dream was still weird. She is finally prepared to go to work. Her and her parent use the train for transportation. Only the rich and wealthy own vehicles. Everything that has to do with work, entertainment, education can be found in the Inwards. Their work hours are contrary to one other. When Courtney is leaving home, Janice is returning home. Being a few minutes behind, Janice was home drinking coffee already. Rushing to catch the train in time, she greeted her parent with a hug.

"Good morning. I will be in late tonight, so don't wait up for me."

"Umm, I have to work tonight so I will not be home either. So, what's going on to keep you out late on a Thursday night? I know you rushing and you have to go but are you finally going on a date?"

Courtney always shies away from this conversation. She feels so out of place. All her life she hasn't been attracted to any fems. That's why her social life is almost nonexistent.

"No, I'm not going on a date. I'm going out with Lacey. She wants to go to the club and meet up with some prospects."

Janice starts laughing. Lacey is always with a different fem.

"Prospect? Lacey needs to slow her ass down. I'm not her parent or anything but she has a new prospect every week!"

Courtney sips a small amount of Janice coffee.

"I told her about that too, but she doesn't listen. Well, I will see you later. Be safe and I love you."

She responded by signing, 'I love you too'. Courtney has no clue what she is saying or doing when she does that and neither does Brandy.

Living in the Inwards had its perks however just like the rest of Femdom, there is crime, drugs, entitlement, and pride. Usually, Courtney meets Lacey on the train but today she sat alone. She anxiously looked around waiting to see her running to the train stop. There are not a lot of commuters that take the train this early in the morning. Two other fems that take the train daily are in her section. Lacey and Courtney secretly make fun of them. One of them is noticeably short. Her height isn't what they find amusing, it's the thick line of hair over her lip. This type of facial hair was rare in Femdom. Lacey made fun of how strange her voice sound also. The fem that is with her is totally opposite. She is tall, dresses nice and always have her makeup on point. Today they sat in the seat behind Courtney.

The short one did most of the talking. She leaned forward and tapped Courtney on the shoulder.

"How are you doing this morning?"

Courtney noticed a Web tattoo on her hand. Those that affiliated with Web were known to be troublemakers.

"I'm good."

Courtney turned around and went back to minding her own business.

"I see your friend not on the train with you today."

Courtney turned around and looked at her. It took everything in her to stop herself from laughing. All she could see was the hair over her lip.

"Yeah, she must be running late today."

### 

Back at Lacey's apartment, one of her new prospects is hindering her from leaving. She is standing in the doorway wearing an oversized t-shirt while hiding Lacey's keys behind her back. Lacey is fully dressed and late for work. She reassures her that they will continue where they left off as she attempts to wrestle the keys from her. They ended up eye to eye at the front door. Lacey wraps her arms around her and whispers,

"Shae, you going to make me late for work. I spent all night with you, give me my keys so I can go."

Her friend is turned on sensually. She slowly bites her lip.

"I don't want you to leave me," she whispers.

She rubs her breast against Lacey's uniform shirt. Lacey places one hand in the small of her back and the other hand cuffing her ass and passionately kissing her. She slowly freed her of the t-shirt as the keys fell, bouncing on the carpet. Lacey turns her around and squeezed her breast while bruising her neck with hickeys. Her index and middle finger teamed simultaneously as they traveled across the freshly cut diamond. The wetness of her desire showered the tips of her fingers. They both panted like a marathon was ran. She gripped Lacey's hand with the inner strength of her thighs as she trembled across the finish line.

Time was up. Lacey was really late. She has already been written up several times on the job for tardies.

"Aria, what time is it", she asked her IT.

"It is 6:17am", Aria replied.

Lacey started rushing Shae. She literally grabbed a shirt and put it over her head.

"Babe put on some clothes really quick and drop me off. I can't show up late again. My supervisor talking about writing me up."

Shae slipped on some clothes while Lacey waited impatiently at the door. This was one way of getting her guest out the house. She would say that she is late and need a ride. In reality, she doesn't want to put them out, so she creates these last-minute scenarios, but today she was late for real.

### 

Now Courtney is on the train stuck in a conversation with hairy lip. She is hoping for the stop to appear magically to free her of this morning dialogue. She did learn the names of the two fems. The tall one name was Azavia, and the talker went by a nickname Shortie. Shortie started to ask

Courtney uncomfortable questions about the law. Azavia remained silent.

"See, I don't agree with that. Laws should be made to keep order but not to control fems. They built walls and no one questioned their motive."

Courtney was tired of the constant rebuttals.

"That's what I love about the world of Femdom, we are all allowed to own our own views and opinions. Even fems in other countries are on the same playing field of equality. Just last year in the Asian territories of Japan, those fems came together and tore down centuries of oppression. It was all on the news. Just like our city, there were many people that were against the walls that separate us from the Outwards."

Shortie jumped in and out of the conversation at will. She had problems with those that didn't agree with her view points.

"Yeah, both my parents fought to keep the gate down. The Orders wasn't trying to protect us from a contagious illness or violent people. They are fems like us. It was built to silence their view of the Orders control."

The train slowed down. Courtney was excited to finally be delivered from this town hall conversation that Shortie started and wants to end it. Courtney being who she is, will let her have the last word.

"'It was nice to have officially met you two. Have a good day."

Shortie said," It was nice meeting you too, think about what I said though. The wall wasn't created to keep the Outwards out but to lock us in. They send us to school to teach us their truth but the truth about femdom is beyond the walls of every city."

Courtney shook her head in agreement but the voice in her head was saying, "Fem, shut the fuck up."

The train stopped and they exited, splitting ways. Oxicure was only two blocks from the warehouse district that Azavia and Shortie were headed too. Shortie saw that they were running a little late for work.

"Come on, we can't be late every damn day. It doesn't take that long to get ready."

Azavia stayed silent. They walked to the back of one of the warehouses. This warehouse was positioned next to a parking garage. Most of the residents commuted by train so this building always went unnoticed. Shortie pressed the intercom button next to the outside entrance door. The voice that replied was very pleasant, sweetness of an older fem.

" How can I assist you today?"

Shortie replied, "It's me, Shortie."

They were buzzed into the warehouse. The interior did not compare to the exterior of the building. This place was beautiful. The entrance foyer was dressed with what looked to be ancient oil paintings. The floors were covered with large Italian etched tiles. There was a receptionist desk that guarded the main entrance into the warehouse. The lights from a giant chandelier radiated reminiscent of the stars at midnight. This place was magnificent. There was a name on the large rug directly under the chandelier, Twilight.

Twilight was designed as an escort service. In reality, it was more like a sex trafficking brothel. The receptionist with the sweet voice is known as Fem Madam. This practice has been undetected from authorities for years. Fems from the Outwards were snuck through the wall and given an opportunity to make money and get food for their families as a tradeoff for sex. The Outwards lived their lives without the stamp, so it was impossible to obtain a job in the Inwards. Shortie had no idea that one of Azavia clients owned a chain of grocery stores. That is how she supplied food to the Outwards from her home/shop. Azavia really had a heart for people. She didn't enjoy the trade she was making but felt it was worth the sacrifice.

Fem Madame gave Azavia a lanyard with her number hanging from it. As they walked into what looked like a ballroom, they were met by other beautiful fems of different ages. They all had numbers around their necks.

All the elite fems, executives, and company owners have a catalog of fems that they can order. The Twilight has individual pods that is used when needed for lunch breaks or quick visits. Cars are sent to transport these fems to whatever place is requested by the client.

Shortie has been Azavia's procuress for about 8 months now. Shortie, along with some of her friends from the Web often traveled to and from the wall. Some of Web followers over time have gotten the stamp. Others have traditional views about the Orders control and rebelled against the stamp. Every time Web gets together, its historically for no good reason. Shortie and her sect were in the Outwards looking for Remnants. Remnants have been used as punching bags since their origin. All around Femdom, they love to afflict violence on the Remnant because they feel they are weak, religious freaks. This particular day, Shortie's attention was taken by Azavia, she was helping some local fems with hygiene products and things of that sort. Because of her beauty, Shortie knew how profitable she would be. It was already on Azavia's mind to find a new way to bring in food to the Outwards, she was afraid to go without protection. She heard of the Twilights reputation of enslaving fems. Shortie propositioned her and she immediately accepted.

The mornings that Azavia work, Shortie hung around until her first appointment is set. She never knows the names of the fems she meets. Depending on the number of appointments, Shortie hung out in the Inwards with friends until the Twilight send her a notification, informing her that Azavia's shift is complete.

### 

Lacey on the other hand has just been dropped off to Oxicure. Oxicure was the only multifaceted security company during that time. Those employed at this location were given zones of the city to monitor. The Order also used Oxicure to monitor the walls so the Outwards would not breach. The employee's duty was to sit in front of the assigned zones and monitor all activity. Those subscribed had the option of turning the audio off or on. It was against policy to override the audio. Most of the customers kept the audio on. It was funny to the workers especially when audio is on, and someone is having sex. Who wanted to hear that at work.

Now Courtney has made it to work and there is still no sign of Lacey. She heard about the write ups and knew she was walking on thin ice. She sent her a projected text.

" Where r you?"

Lacey heard the text and viewed it on her glasses. She sends her an audio text.

"I'm here!"

Lacey made it on time. Her supervisor Rebecca stood by the bio clock waiting.

"Ok Lacey, you were almost late again!"

Lacey is known for having a smart mouth.

"First of all, we all grown in here, so why are you waiting at the clock. Your screen in your office will tell you the same time I clock in. Secondly, there is no such thing as almost late Rebecca. That's like someone saying they almost won a game, how? How can you almost win? You either win or you lose, you either on time or you are late."

She stepped closer like she was going to kiss her and whispered in her ear.

"You either my prospect or you are not."

Rebecca got upset and stormed off. Oh, I guess you figured out that Lacey has done more at work than monitor security.

Courtney shook her head as Lacey grabbed her assignment and sat in a chair next to her.

"Your ass is crazy fem. Why you didn't catch the train this morning...you know what, I don't think I want to know. I bet it's about some prospect. You left me alone to talk to hairy lip."

Lacey was shocked, "Hairy lip? I'm gone for one day and you find some new friends?" They both start laughing.

"No, that isn't my new friend. She asked about you and started talking about all this militant bullshit."

"I don't know why she asked about me. Short with hair on the face isn't my type. What zones did revengeful ass Rebecca give you today?"

"She gave me all the quiet zones of the city."

Lacey was playfully upset. She wanted to see was Rebecca being petty or not.

"Oh, this is how she act. She only doing this shit because I scratched her off my list. She gave you zones 5,7,8, 13, see, she is being petty! That's all my areas. I should go in her office and put my hand on her screen and show her this baddy I had last night."

She actually paused as if she was thinking about it.

"I'm about to go in there and tell her she can't kiss. I know that will piss her off!"

Courtney stopped her, "Sit your ass down and leave Rebecca alone. You had that fem leave her Union thinking she had something with you."

Lacey got defensive, "I never told her to leave her union. Her union wanted me to unite with them."

Courtney turned her chair toward her monitors.

"You are crazy. I'm going to work my easy zones and relax. My mind will be free. I hope you will be ready to go out tonight."

"What are you talking about, its Thursday and we off for the whole weekend, yeah, I'm ready. I'm going to get you tore up tonight. We going to that new spot Aces. I have two hot fems that will meet us."

Lacey said as she sat in her chair. Courtney became very anxious. She didn't know how to tell Lacey that she isn't attracted to fems like that.

"I'm good, I'm cool, I'm not trying to meet none of your prospects. I just want to get out and have fun. My parent even saying I need to get out more."

Lacey and Courtney had a fairly good day at work. They only had two hours left on the clock. One of Courtneys zones had a suspicious activity alert. Zone 8 was the home of one of the cities elite judges. Her name is Camilla. She normally stays to herself. Not a real fan of society. She lives her life introvertly. What made the alert go off was a black car that circled her driveway twice. Any unusual action that identITy senses, an activity alert is sent to Oxicure. Courtney switches the camera to the interior view. It shows the judge getting out the shower. While she gets dressed, Courtney gets another alert but this time it's in Zone 5. She takes her headset off and turn to Lacey who is half sleep.

"We need to switch zones when we come back to work Monday. This is too much stuff going on in these zones for me."

Lacey mumbled," This shit boring, I'm ready to get out of here."

Another alert sounds in Zone 5. Courtney was not use to this at all.

"Look at this shit, some bad ass children pushing over trash containers."

Lacey leaned over and grabbed Courtneys headset off her head. The city used Oxicure services also. Cameras with audio was mounted under the streetlights especially in the upper-class sides of town. Lacey accessed the speaker closes to the children that were running.

"Emily, Justin, and you with the red shirt, STOP! We know exactly where you live and who your parents are. So, what I need you to do, is go back and pick up all the trash that you knocked over or I will send this video to your homes and watch as your parents whoop your ass."

Courtney took her headset from her. Lacey started laughing. Rebecca came out her office.

"Lacey, I need to speak to you in my office, now!"

She left her section and walked toward her office.

"I know you not mad because I made those bad ass children clean up that mess."

Rebecca replied as she closed her door," You have to follow protocol. When has profanity ever been a part of protocol Lacey?"

Courtney turns her attention back to Zone 8. The judge stood at her front door with what looked like a robe. She was anticipating a guest it seemed. A well-dressed fem got out the back seat and walked to the door. Courtney tried to be nosey by switching cameras to get a better view. There was no way to see her face, but she was dressed in a blue glittery evening gown. What really stood out was the diamond studded silver heels she stepped in. The judge was kind of frisky that evening. The way she greeted her was as if her guest was dessert. She waved off the car's driver. Her audio and video remained on so Courtney listened.

"Come in and have a seat and I will get you something to drink."

This was her guest first time being there. Her eyes were like a young filly.

"Your home is very nice, do you play the piano? I always wanted to learn how to play!"

The judge poured her a glass of wine and walked over to the couch she sat on. She opened her robe and exposed her naked desire.

"You are not here to talk about my belongings, open your mouth."

She poured the wine in her mouth. Some of the wine escaped along her chin and the judge licked it up. She then straddled her guest as they kissed.

By this time Lacey came back to her desk.

She whispered, "I am ready to get out of here".

Courtney replied," Me too. I don't want to monitor your zones anymore. Children acting up, the judge trying to get some…"

Lacey spit out the water she was drinking.

"What, let me see!"

Courtney pans the camera to locate the two, she was unsuccessful.

"They were just on the couch kissing, where did they go! See you probably thinking I'm making all this up, but I know what I saw."

Lacey told her to navigate to each room in the house, but she still couldn't find the two. Lacey started to think that they were playing a game of hide and seek. When they still couldn't see them in the house, Lacey told her to try the basement.

"There they go Lacey, damn, her basement look as good as the rest of the house. Yep, they still at it. I'm not going to watch this."

"Shit, I am!"

Rebecca made a noise to clear her throat as she watched Lacey from her office door. Lacey looked at her, rolled her eyes and moved back to her seat. There were no other alerts on Courtney's Zones. Without alerts, Oxicure has no legal right to the video or audio.

Courtney was looking at the clock and only had an hour remaining. An alert went off again in Zone 8. Her identITy responded to the screams of her guest.

"Camilla, are you ok? Do your guest need medical attention? Her heart rate is dropping and her oxygen levels are declining."

"No Amy, my guest does not need medical attention. I need you to deactivate until morning."

Amy said, "Good night", and shut down.

What the judge didn't realize is that her system shut down but once an alert goes out to Oxicure, their cameras stay on. The judge covered her guest mouth to muzzle the screams as she penetrated her with something that look like a flimsy cucumber. Her guest screamed.

"Stop please, that hurts!"

The judge opened her legs and got on top of her in a scissored position. She grinded on her until her screams turned to moans of pleasure. Before they both reached the height of their engagement, the judge placed her hand around her throat and started violently choking her. Courtney jumped up from her chair and called Rebecca. She was frantic.

"Do I cut of the feed, or ask do she need help or send a patrol car, what do I do?"

Rebecca attempted to calm her down. She had to grab her and softly rub her hands up and down her arms.

"Take a deep breath and tell me what is going on."

"The judges' alert went off again in Zone 8. It alerted use because of screaming in the basement. She shut her alarm off, but our system remained active, and now she is choking her."

Rebecca checked the monitor, but Zone 8 camera was off.

"The camera to Zone 8 is off Courtney!"

She looks at the monitor and was baffled that it was off.

"I know what I just watched. She was choking her, and her guest was trying to fight back!"

"Ok, listen Courtney, by policy, you can ask if she need assistance since we were alerted but other than that, there is nothing we can do."

Courtney got on the speaker for Zone 8.

"This is Oxicure, we received an alert from your home, do you need help?"

There was silence. Camilla didn't respond at all. Courtney tried again.

"This is Oxicure, we received an alert from your home, do you need help? Do I need to send a patrol car?"

When the judge heard her mention a patrol car, she quickly replied, "No, everything is just fine. I'm just getting ready for bed."

She cut the cameras back on as she removed the extra pillows from her comforter. She even waved at the camera to show that she was ok. Rebecca pulled Courtney to the side.

"The judge looks ok, and she just said that she was safe so that is what you write on the alert report. That frees Oxicure of all liability."

Courtney was shaken up. She has been with Oxicure for years and have never had a day like this.

"I know what I saw on the camera. She invited that lady over and choked her!"

Rebecca pulled her in the office, "The longer you work here the more things you will see that is disturbing. You just have to make sure you go according to protocol. Sometimes you have to learn to untrust what you see."

"How do I do that! I guess I have to learn how to lie to myself. Is that what you telling me?"

"Sometimes your eyes lie to you. If you see something that you have to prove, it's probably because it was a lie in the first place."

Courtney was confused. She stood in the doorway of Rebecca's office trying to really make sense out of what just happened or what she thought she saw happen.

"Courtney, before you clock out, make sure you close out all your zones and make reports on the alerts for your shift."

She went to her desk and closed out her zones. Before closing out Zone 8, she noticed that the cameras were off at the judge's house. She tapped into the cities pole camera in front of Camilla's home. That same black car was backed into the driveway. This time three fems got out and went to the door. Lacey started rushing Courtney because she had all she could take that day. Courtney reassured her that she was almost finished. She looked back at the camera and two of the fems were carrying what looked like a stuffed sleeping bag out the house. She whispered to Lacey.

"Come look at this shit. I told you something is going on!"

Thy stuffed the bag in the trunk of the car. The other fem shakes the judge's hand and got into the back seat of the car and left. Lacey look Courtney straight in the eye.

"I know you had a long day; we both had a long day. Close out zone 8 and let's get ready to go out, you hear me, let's go!"

She closed out the zone and they left.

Courtney was distracted as her and Lacey waited on the train to go home and get dressed. Lacey is being her normal talkative self while Courtney mind is still at work. Lacey was the first to notice Shortie walking toward the train stop.

"There goes your fem, Courtney."

Before she could turn her head, Shortie was calling out to her.

"Hey Courtney, how long have you been waiting on the train?"

"We just got here about 5 minutes ago, why, what's going on?"

"Have you seen Azavia? I wasn't notified when she got off work and her building in the warehouse district is closed. All the lights were off, and no one is answering the intercom."

Lacey saw that Courtney night is almost a total lost if she doesn't get focused.

"Damn, we sorry to hear about your fem. If we see her, we will holla at you."

Shortie thanked them and walked away. She was headed back down to the warehouse district.

### 

Its 9:30pm and all the drinks are free until midnight. The music is loud, and the Aces is packed. As soon as Courtney and Lacey arrived, they had the bartender pour them two drinks. Lacey had fems all over her. She was a fem magnet. Courtney actually enjoyed watching Lacey interact with the fems. She saw her more like her alter ego. If she was attracted to fems, she would be just like her. The only problem is, she is not like her. Being out in crowds was exhausting for Courtney. She would rather be home in the comfort of her home watching Teen Love.

As Courtney sat alone at the bar, a fem name Vanessa came and sat next to her.

"Hey, what's your name?"

Courtney looked around to see exactly who she was talking too. She realized that she was the only one at the bar. She took a deep breath and tried to loosen up and be more open.

"I'm Courtney. What's your name?"

"I'm Vanessa. I saw you at another club a few times, but I was too nervous to talk to you."

Courtney was bashful with a tablespoon of shyness. She haven't met to many fems with the same measurements before.

"Why are you nervous? You are a beautiful fem."

"Thank you but I never approached a fem and just the thought of it causes me anxiety. I'm really shy but tonight I said to myself, after I had a few drinks, I was going ask someone to dance with me. Then I saw you sitting here. It took everything in me to ask, so here I am. Courtney would you like to dance with me?"

Courtney started laughing, "I'm not the best dancer but we can try."

They got out on the dance floor and danced for what seemed like hours. After a few more drinks and a couple more dances, Courtneys night went black. The next light she saw was the next morning when she woke up in bed with Vanessa.

# 2

The Remnant lived mostly in cities with tunnels and abandoned substations. They traveled beneath the cities in order to avoid persecution. Each sect wore a different colored Monk habit. Those that defended the compounds also wore the cowl to cover their face in public. Every so often they come up for air with a message to the Outwards to trust in God or die without God.

All the holy books have been destroyed around Femdom. In the eastern section of the City of New Daphne, there is a total of eight elders and 47 fem followers. The Remnant depends on the Elders memory to guide the people. The only problem is, the Elders have forgotten as much as they remembered over the past 40 yrs. The younger Remnant's move different from how they were taught. These group of fems doesn't turn the other cheek, they fight back.

Food is getting scarce for the Remnant. They are not allowed in the city, so they have to find food in the Outwards. The Outwards would not have a problem helping if they weren't so entangled in the Web. For years, Friday has normally been the day that Elder Anna sent out their young leaders to get food and supplies. Elder Anna was the voice for her sect. Bria is one of the leaders. She normally takes her younger sibling and 3 others when they go up top for supplies. Bria sister name is Lisa. Lisa is lazy and never want to do anything. The other three names are Tiffany, Teja and Tonya. They are tough fems. Tiffany and Teja are siblings. They followed their parent Bonnie and was trained in mixed martial arts but the Remnant is known to be nonviolent, so their abilities were suppressed. Bonnie died when they were no older than 10. This was during the time when those that lacked melanin in their skin started to die without cause. Doctors said it was because those that have high levels of melanin skin converts the sun's rays into energy. Those with the least melanin, the sun's rays became radiation and their bodies burned from the inside out. Whatever the cause may be, a lot of people died. It almost wiped out all those that had clear skin. Before the Virus, most of these clear skinned people began to mix with melanin people in order to survive. It was like they knew that day was coming.

Back to the story, It normally takes the five of them about two hours to reach the store for supplies.

Bria woke up Lisa, "Come on fem, we have been chosen by the Elders."

Lisa rolls over on the pallet she sleeps on. She was tired from sleeping.

"Leave me alone and why you making it sound so sheroic, 'we have been chosen by the elders!" We have be chosen every week Bria. Tell the Elders to go get their own stuff, I'm tired. Its good exercise for those old legs of theirs."

Bria pulled the cover off her," Tired from what, you don't do anything. You always sitting here in this same spot isolated from everyone."

Lisa sat up on her pallet," You are right, I stay right here and mind my business. I don't bother anybody. This is the lane I travel. I don't even go across anyone's lane because I learned how-to live-in mine. With all that being said, why do you want me to go and get some stupid supplies"?

"I want you to go with me because you are my only sibling, and I don't want anything to happen to you."

Lisa became sarcastic, "Nothing will happen to me because I'm staying right here in my bed."

The three T's walked into the room, Tiffany asked Bria," Is Lisa trying to stay here again?"

Bria was disappointed, "Yes like always."

Teja encouraged Bria to let her stay," She will just slow us done because she doesn't want to be here. Us four can go and get everything we need and be back by lunchtime."

Lisa covered her head with her blanket, "That is a great idea Teja. I will be right here in this exact spot when you all get back. Oh yeah, don't worry about the Elders, I will keep them safe along with the 40 plus other fems that live down here."

The four started their journey.  Bria was uneasy about leaving her but she didn't want to hear her complaining the entire way. Now one fem that went with them was a complainer that that was Tonya. She never understood why the Remnant didn't join with the Outwards.

"It just doesn't make sense to me. We are going to the Outwards so we can fill our backpacks up with their food, but we can't live with them because….?"

Bria tried to explain, "The Elders said they were getting persecuted by everyone because they believed in God. God was said to have created where we live and created a place for use to live in the afterlife. They called us stupid and started attacking us. Everyone that believed this way hid because they didn't want to use the same violence that those that persecuted used."

Tiffany got upset, "The Elders made us sound like some scary ass fems. Somebody doesn't like you, so you run and hide. That makes no sense. If you don't like me, it's your fault not mine. Why would we give them that much power over our lives? How do you expect the Outwards, Orders, and even the Inwards to take us seriously and the first thing they did in the old world was run and hide in some dark holes in the cities? All around Femdom, in every country, Remnants are known as religious hiders."

Bria was the peacekeeper in the group, "Maybe hiding was how they survived so they can preserve the history."

Tiffany anger was heightened, "Survive, that's what you call this? We are living like peasants. We have to sneak around and beg for food all in the name of God. The Elders can't even remember what they trying to preserve…."

"Be quiet," Teja heard a noise.

She told everyone to get against the wall and to be totally silent. She pulled a machete out of her habit. The other fems pulled out metal poles. They all covered their faces with their cowls.

Bria was shocked, "Damn, where did you get a big ass knife from?"

Teja started smiling, "This old thing, it's a part of my knife collection now be quiet."

This section of the tunnels was called the Shadows. It is a four-way track that meet in the center of the tunnels. This is where traps are normally set for Remnants and others living below the city. They stealthily disappeared as the stepped deeper into the Shadows. The more the Shadows concealed their presence the less the tunnels protected the Webs presence. Bria spotted 8 to 10 Web members headed their way.

She whispers, "Let's go back, its too many of them!"

They silently agreed with her by their actions. As they began to take slow backwards steps, Tiffany stopped.

Bria asked her, "What are you doing, let's go?"

The Web got closer and closer. They were able to interpret their conversations. Tiffany was tired of running.

"I'm tired of putting my tail between my legs and running from low life pieces of shit like the Web."

Bria urges her to retreat," Let's find another way Tiffany!"

Tiffany stepped out on the track where the dim lights hung.

She looked over at Bria, "I'm tired of finding another way. It's time to fight". She yells at the Web members," Are you all looking for the Remnant, here we go!"

The Web members couldn't believe it. They were looking for trouble and they found it. They ran towards Tiffany thinking that she was going to retreat. Tonya and the other two stepped out of the Shadow and assisted in initiating this brawl. Teja spotted the first fem running toward Tiffany. She did a round house kick that landed, spot on, the side of her head. Before she hit the ground, Teja used the machete and swung it in the direction of the second fem. It cut the string from her hoodie and barely sliced across her chest. Teja grabbed the back of her head as she reached for her chest and kneed her in the nose. This was the first time that any one from Remnant challenged anyone to a fight.

They defended themselves flawlessly. Bria had a fem on the ground, punching her in the face. She looked up and Teja was standing over one of them with the machete raised.

   Bria's voice echoed through the tunnel. "Nooooo, we only kill if it's necessary."

Teja slowly put the knife in its sleeve. The Web members were bloody, injured and battered. They helped each other off the ground and ran down one of the tunnels. The four Remnants stared at each other for a minute. No one said a word. Bria signed, 'Good job', to all of them. They shook their head and continued to the store in Outward.

### ###

It is almost 11am and Courtney is still in bed sleep. She has become paralyzed to this reoccurring dream. She found herself hiding behind a monument in Outwards Park again. This dark hairy figure with the voice of thunder, continues to call her name. This time when she peaks around the monument, she not only hears the monster call her name but also, he's making hand gestures that she doesn't understand. The scariest part in this dream was when she felt the monster grab her hand and rub it across the name on the monument. Out of fear she screamed herself woke.

"Are you ok Courtney? Your oxygen levels seem a little low and your heart rate is rising. Do you need medical attention?"

"No Brandy. I need some water and some more sleep. What time did I get in last night?"

"Courtney, you did not arrive home last night. You and your guest time of entry was at 4:17am".

"What do you mean me and my guest?"

She turned around and there was a fully dressed fem in her bed. She jumped up from the bed and made sure she had clothes on. After making sure she was ok she shook her guest to wake her.

"Hey, excuse me, you have to wake up."

Her guest woke up just as surprised as Courtney did. She stood up and checked herself.

"We didn't do anything last night, did we?"

Courtney nervously replied, "I don't know. All I remember was…damn, I don't remember anything, shit. Wait, I can ask Brandy. Brandy did me and, what's your name again?"

She replied", Vanessa, damn she don't even remember my name."

She starts to look for her shoes and the rest of her belongings.

"Brandy, did me and Vanessa do anything when we entered the house this morning?"

"Yes, you went to the restroom to vomit. I then asked do you need medical attention and your words to me were, Shut the fuck up. You always asking do I need… pause…vomit, moan in pain, vomit some more."

"Okay Brandy, that's too much information. What I need to know is, did me and Vanessa kiss or have sex?"

"No. You two took off your shoes and fell asleep until you were awakened by the monster at the monument."

"How did you know what was in my dream this morning?"

Vanessa just put her shoes on, "Courtney, I'm sorry but how do I get out of here, I'm so embarrassed."

Courtney consoled her, "Don't be embarrassed. I'm glad we made it home safely because I don't remember shit."

While they talked, Courtney phone rung," Hold on Vanessa, Hello."

It was Lacey calling her, "Heads up, Tameka and Freda are no call, no shows at work. Rebecca will be calling you in a little while, bye."

Courtney looked at her palm and shook her head, "Where do you live? I probably have to go to work. I can't believe no one showed up to work on the weekend."

Vanessa thought about what Courtney said and remembered that she had to be at work at 2pm.

"Oh shit, I have to go home and get ready for work too. I forgot it was Friday. Where are we?"

"You are on the east side of the. Where do you work?"

"I'm a Central Police Officer," Vanessa replied.

"You don't look like a police officer. Now I'm thinking, how do police look."

They both start laughing.

Vanessa asked, "Can you walk me out and can I get your number?"

Courtney put her shoes on to walk her downstairs, "Yeah that's cool. Can I be honest with you?"

"I hope so," Vanessa replied.

"I don't like going out because I don't like fems like that. What I'm saying is..."

Vanessa mirrored her response, "You not attracted to fems like that, me either."

They were excited to finally meet someone that felt the same way. They exchanged numbers and Courtney was walking her out when they walked past Janice in the kitchen.

"Hello, ok this is different! Good morning, how you are doing Courtney. Who is your guest"?

"Parent, Vanessa, Vanessa this is my parent Janice."

Vanessa hugged Janice, "Nice to meet you Janice."

She gave Courtney a hug also and left to catch the train. When the door closed, you could hear a pin drop in their home. Courtney literally started sweating and having a panic attack.

Brandy said, "Courtney, are you feeling okay, your heart rate…"

Courtney responded by saying," Brandy shut up, you always asking do I need help. You always know my dreams so why you don't help me to understand it?"

Brandy got technical, "I was programmed to be security, a friend and someone that you could talk to. Some answers I can't give you because it would violate the Orders memory Act of 2042."

Janice asked Courtney, "Are you still having dreams about that monster?"

"Yes, they haven't stopped, I tried everything, but the dream keeps reoccurring. I think I need to see a specialist for real."

Her parent consoled her, "You don't need a specialist. Most of the time when a dream keep coming to you in the same form, it means it's something you need to do."

"That's the problem. I don't know what I need to do. This morning, that monster called my name and did something with its hands," Courtney explained.

"Ok, show me what it did with its hands". Courtney attempts the signs that the monster did after calling her name in the dream."

Janice was in shock, "Were the signs more like this……"

Courtney was excited, "Yes just like that! How did you know what was done? It's like everyone knows what is going on in my dream but me."

Janice changed the subject, "We will talk about it at a later time. Now tell me about your guest. How did you meet, and do you like her, what's going on?"

"Vanessa is just like me, we don't like fems but we did have fun hanging out, I think. I don't really remember."

While she was in mid conversation, the phone rang, it's her supervisor Rebecca. Rebecca asked could she possibly work and extra shift, Courtney agreed. While she was taking a shower and prepared for work, Janice looked for a cloth or paper to write on. Paper and pencil were obsolete, old way, considered a thing of the past. Screens and projected technology was the future. Technology made it possible to text, send notes or letters via Emessage. The problem with that was everything was stored in a data base and the Order as privy to it. A lot of the older fems held on to things that even identITy couldn't recognize. They couldn't interpret Jaz sign language and writing on dead surfaces. Janice used some eye liner and a folded piece of cardboard and wrote this message to Courtney.

"The signs you saw in your dreams said, Find the doctor and you will find me."

As she prepared to leave, Janice put the cardboard in her pocket and told her to look at it later, she agreed. On the way to work, Courtney was feeling a little displaced. She wasn't used to taking the train to work alone. She looked around and she didn't recognize any of these commuters. Trying to find something that would occupy her time on the train, she remembered that her mom gave her a note. She secretly pulled it out her pocket and read it.

"Find the doctor and you will find me," she was confused.

What does that mean, find the doctor and you will find me? She is lost and she is thinking her mom has some screws loose too. As the train slows, she passed Shortie walking aimlessly towards the train stop. As soon as the doors opened, Courtney darted in her direction calling her name. She was out of breath by the time she caught up with her.

Courtney was breathing heavy, "Hey, did you ever find Azavia?"

Shortie immediately started crying, "No, she never came home." She pulled Courtney to the side," Don't tell anyone but Azavia is an Outwards. I sneak her in to make money so she can feed the poor in the Outwards. She has been working in the warehouse district for almost a year. Every day she is in and out like clockwork until yesterday. All of a sudden, they didn't notify me when she was done".

Courtney was concerned, "I work at Oxicure so when I'm on the monitors today, I will see if I can see her." Shortie thanked her.

"Wait, what did she have on yesterday?"

Shortie thought about it, "She wore this short black skirt that morning. If you see her, please let me know. Courtney, I forgot she changed that evening. She put on a blue shiny long dress with some shiny ass shoes. She said that outfit made her feel like a movie star, damn, I need to find her."

Courtney was almost late, so she rushed to work. She clocked in and received her zones for the day.

### 

Shortie put a lot of miles on her shoes looking for Azavia. It was impossible to call because those in the Outwards wasn't allowed to have phones. She walked back to the warehouse. Shortie pressed the buzzer and Fem Madam answered.

"How may I help you today?"

Shortie aggressively answered, "You can stop all the bullshit and tell me where Azavia is!"

Madam pleasantly replied, "If you have a catalog, you can order which ever fem you desire. I am pretty sure we have a few fems with that name. All Twilights' catalogs are updated weekly."

Shortie temper has hit overload, "I don't think you know who the fuck you are playing with. I'm a General in the Web. I will burn this place to the fucking ground! Where is Azavia?"

Madam asked Shortie nicely, "If you do not have a catalog, I'm asking you to leave the premises."

Shortie became very irate. She began to kick the door and yell obscenities. Madam buzzed her in. As soon as Shortie slung the door open, she was greeted by two large fems. The average height for a fem was 5'5. These two fems stood at about six feet. They looked like all they did in their spare time was lift weights. One of them threw Shortie to the ground and both of them took turns punching and kicking her. Shortie pleaded with them to stop but her pleas were ignored. After several minutes of getting beat, Fem Madam stepped in between the fems with a gun in her hand.

She put the gun to Shorties head, "Let me tell you something, I don't take kindly to threats. Don't you ever come to my fucking establishment that I built with my bare hands and threaten to burn it to the ground. I will kill everyone you love while you watch and then I will make u watch me put a bullet in between your fucking eyes. Do you understand me?"

Shortie shamefully said, "Yes."

Madam screamed directly in her ear. "DO YOU UNDERSTAND ME!"

"YES, I understand you, I'm sorry. I'm sorry."

The two fems drug her out the front door and pushed her to the ground. One of them showed Shortie a Web tattoo on her hand.

"Look like we have the same tattoo Shortie. Let me tell you something. I'm a fucking General in the Web so I know you lying about your ranking. You don't have enough soldiers under you. At the end of the day, none of that shit even matter around here. Bring your ass back to the Outwards with that weak shit. The only people that fear Web is the old ass Elders of the Remnant and I will be scavenging their shit in a little while. Get out of here and don't bring your little ass back here again."

They shut the door and told Madam that they will not have any more problems out of her. Madam sat down at her desk and cut her PV on.

"She almost made me miss my show."

### ###

It is after 2pm and Lacey is in the kitchen making lunch. Shae just received a text from her parent. She walks in the kitchen with nothing on but a pair of Lacey's socks.

Lacey was speechless, "Shae, you must don't believe in wearing clothes?"

Shae hugs Lacey and whispers in her ear, "Not around you. You make me want to take my clothes off every time I'm around you."

Lacey passionately kisses her, "I have some lunch made if you are hungry."

"I am hungry, but I have to go. My parent need me to come down to the office. She said they had an issue and want me to come in for a while. My parent really want me to take over her business but I want to find my own way. Not live in her shadow."

Lacey replied, "If my parent had the money your parent have, forget what I want to do, I'm taking over the business."

They both laughed.

"I wanna make a deal with you. If I put some clothes on, can I come see you later?"

Lacey smiled, "That's cool. My fem Courtney have to work so I will be by myself this evening anyway."

Shae got dressed and left. Lacey was at home bored, she started texting Courtney.

"What time do you get off today? She replied.

"Leave me alone Lacey. How did you let me leave the club with someone I didn't even know."

Lacey was confused, "What are you talking about, I do that shit all the time!"

Before Courtney could respond, she received a text from Vanessa. "Hey, I hope I'm not bothering you but I just wanted to tell you that I had a great time last night, well the part I remember."

Courtney started smiling, "Me too. What are you doing right now?"

"I was called to a crime scene on your side of the tracks. I haven't gotten there yet but I will let you know about it later," Vanessa replied.

Courtney was excited about her new friend, "Ok, be safe out there."

### 

By this time, Bria and her team confidently made it to the place where they collected their supplies. Because they are not welcomed by so many Outwards, they had to move surreptitious. The owner of the shop normally has their supplies in the back so they can walk through the alley and retrieve it unnoticed. They walked through the alley and heard voices coming from behind the fence at the shop.

Tonya peaked through a hole in the fence and whispered to the others, "It's the same fems that we beat up in the Shadows."

Bria couldn't believe it. She peaked through the hole, "What are they doing here? Normally Azavia put out all the supplies, we pay her and then we go. Something got to be going on. Azavia isn't the type to even hang around low life's like the Web."

While they trying to figure out what is going on and why their supplies wasn't packed, someone walked through the house looking for Azavia. It was Shortie. Shortie was battered and beaten like the rest of her crew. When she walked out the back door, Christy noticed that Shortie had gotten into an altercation with someone.

"What happened to you?"

Shortie being sarcastic, "Look like the same thing that happened to me happened to all of you! I got the shit kicked out of me."

Jordan is the fem that Teja cut, she wanted to know what happened to Shortie.

"Who did this to you and why?"

All four of the Remnant team is at the gate listening by this time.

Shortie explains, "Azavia is missing! I have been taking her to Twilight to make some extra money to keep her store going. Last night they didn't notify me that her shift was complete. I went back earlier today, and this is the answer they gave me."

Christy was saddened by what she heard, "That doesn't sound like her at all, I hope nothing happened to her."

Shortie asked, "What happened to all of you?"

Jordan started to tell her side of the story, "We were walking through the tunnel looking for Remnants. They normally show their faces during the weekend. We figured we would catch them slipping and kick their asses. Shortie, they ambushed us. It was about 20 of them. They stomped and kicked us. We barely made it out with our lives."

Bria and the other Remnants started laughing.

Shortie heard the laughter and slowly walked to the gate, "Who is that, show yourself!"

They pulled out their weapons and opened the boarded gate. The eight Web members that were in the subway jumped to their feet in fear.

Jordan came forward, "What do you want, you already cut me?"

Shortie was looking confused, "Where are the rest of your crew that jumped mine?"

Bria responded, "Your fems are lying. It was us four against them. We didn't come here looking for another fight. We came here to meet Azavia."

Shortie became angry as soon as they mentioned her name, "Meet her for what? If you know where she at you better tell me."

Tiffany stepped up to her, "And if we don't tell you where she at, what your short ass going to do?"

Bria pulled her back by her shirt, "First off, we didn't know Azavia was missing. We come and get supplies from her every week. Secondly, if we knew she was associated with trash like you, we would have spent our monies somewhere else. Now that we got that straight, how can we help?"

Christy replied, "When have we ever needed help from the Remnant? All Remnant have ever done was preach garbage about some God that don't give a damn about fems?"

Tension has really starting to stir between them.

Bria came in as the peacekeeper again, "Listen, our beliefs have nothing to do with Azavia's whereabouts. Can we at least put our differences aside so we can figure out what happen to her?"

Everyone stood down. Shortie told everyone all the events that led to her getting beat on at the Twilight.

### 

Courtney is only working part of the shift. She is counting down the minutes to getting off. She had a quiet evening. She even went to Zone 8 to see if the judge had any traffic or alerts, but she didn't. Courtney clocked out and started walking to the train stop.

She got a call from Vanessa, "I'm sorry I didn't get a chance to call you sooner. They had me working on a case with this new fem. Have you ever worked with someone that's new and they already think they know every damn thing."

Courtney replies, "Yep, they hire them all the time at Oxicure".

"Check this out. They found a fem dead this morning at that restaurant on Toronado St. Have you eaten there before?"

Courtney thought about the place for a moment, "Are you talking about the restaurant called, Planters?"

"Yes, they have some good food over there."

Courtney told her that she haven't been there yet but she have heard of it. Vanessa finished telling her what took place earlier that day.

"By the time we got there, the detectives already took pictures and collected all the data they needed from the pole cams. This fem trying to sound important, it must have been a bad drug deal. I looked at her like, fem shut the fuck up. No one doing a drug deal with an expensive ass evening gown and shoes with diamonds in them."

Courtney hand started to shake uncontrollably. The phone call almost disconnected because she didn't keep a constant connection with the glass, she used to project the call.

Courtney voice was trembling, "Did she have on a blue evening gown?"

Vanessa looked at the pictures from the crime scene.

"Yes. How did you know it was blue?"

Courtney walked away from the train stop and continued talking, "Shit, shit, I know what happened to her!"

"Shut up Courtney, don't say anything else. I will meet you at your house in about an hour. Don't say shit to anyone."

Courtney is noticeably shaken, "Okay, I will see you at my house."

# 3

Lisa is laying in the same spot at the camp she was in when Bria left. They didn't have phones, but they had access to PV's. She is sneaking and watching a show. The Elders don't want them watching PV's. They explained to them how the children of old minds were distorted because of TV's. It's getting late and Bria and the others are normally back by this time. Lisa was still unbothered as she watched her show.

There was a loud bang and what sounded like a scream. Lisa cut her PV off. She stood in the doorway and put her shoes on. She thought it was her sibling returning with the supplies. When she walked into the large meeting room where they congregate together. She saw Web gang members ravaging through their things. Elder Anna stood and demanded that they all leave. The leader of this group of Web members was a fem with a chip on her shoulder.

What set her apart was that she was tall and very muscular. She was militant in the way she dealt with the members under her tutelage.

 The lead fem attempted to intimidate the elder," Sit down and shut up!"

 Elder Anna did not back down, "You have no right to be here, especially you. We will not succumb to your violence. The Lord is our shelter, our fortress, it's in God that we put our trust."

The lead fem was getting angry, "I said sit down and shut the fuck up."

 Anna started humming a song directly in her face, 'To God be the glory, to God be the glory, forever and forevermore.'

 Her anger peaked. She grabbed the cane that Elder Anna stood with and hit her several times across her neck and head, "I TOLD YOU TO SHUT UP!"

Lisa watched as the Elder's lifeless body collapsed to the floor. The gang started to savagely beat and tie up everyone in their grasp. Lisa went unnoticed. As quiet as she walked in, was as quiet as she exited. She went back to her room as she contemplated her next move. Lisa had no idea how many there were. Without any bells or alarms, she had no way of alerting the other Remnants. The Web members are now going through the entire compound.

They were looking for religious relics that they can trade for money. Every relic was historic and on the black market, it could buy your way to the Inward. Lisa room started to fill with fear as the walls became transparent. After gathering herself, she went down a back hallway out of the view of the Web. Quickly looking in the rooms along the way, she found no weapons. Teja room was one of the closest. She entered her room looking for a weapon to fight with. Lisa was lazy but she didn't believe in the turn the other cheek teachings from the Elders. Eye for and eye and a tooth for a tooth was a teaching that stuck with her. They just killed one of their elders so now it's time for Lisa to repay the favor.

She pulled a box from under Teja's bed, but it has a pad lock securing it. She looked for something large enough to break the lock. While she searched, the voices of the Web members got closer and louder as they went through the rooms of the compound. Lisa found a metal rod behind the dresser. She tried not to make too much noise as she hit the lock with the rod. The room went silent as she waited to see if they heard her striking the lock, no response. She hit it harder, no response. After the 5th strike, the Web leader heard the strikes echo through the hallway. Their leader counted out six members and sent them to investigate. When she heard that they were on their way, Lisa started banging that lock like her life depended on it. The cautious steps they took turned into running. She finally opened the box and there were several knives. She even found a loaded gun. One of the Web members ran into the room while the others continued to run down the corridor. Lisa grabbed the gun and before she could stand to her feet, the fem lifted a rod to hit her. Lisa fired two shots into her chest from a kneeled position. The impact pushed her backwards through the doorway against the wall in the corridor. Lisa grabbed a knife, closed the box with her foot and pushed it back under the bed. All the fems that ran down the corridor saw was their friend dead and a shadow coming out the room, toward them. Before they could turn around and retreat, Lisa stepped over the fem laying on the floor and shot two others. She then grabbed one of them by the shirt and stabbed her several times. The other two ran out of the compound. The ones that were ravaging through everything didn't ask any questions. When they saw their friends running, they ran with them. Lisa chased them partly down the tunnel. She fired several more rounds in their direction.

"Don't ever bring your asses down here again. I will kill all of you!"

She walked into the compound, and everyone was silent.

###

Bria and her fems sat down for the first time with Web members. They have always been enemies, but Azavia was the common denominator that brought them together. They haven't learned of the news that she was found dead yet. They talked for over an hour and there were no hard feelings over the fight earlier.

Jordan actually joked about it, "We thought we were going to chase some of you down the tunnels like we normally do. Shit, we had no idea the Remnant had a group of super damn sheroes!"

Christy jumped in, "Yeah, your fem Teja standing on the track with that big ass knife. I know I'm not messing with none of you again."

They all laughed. Shortie went into the house and got the supplies they needed.

Bria told Shortie," We will be back next Friday. If you hear back from Azavia by then please let us know."

They shook hands and parted ways.

###

Bria knew it was getting late, so they rushed back to the compound. By this time Courtney just got home. She is a nervous wreck and doesn't know what to do.

As soon as she walks into her home, Janice is sitting on the couch and says, "Courtney we need to talk."

Courtney runs to her parent and give her a long hug. She is crying uncontrollably.

Janice is concerned, "Look at me Courtney, what's wrong baby, what happened?"

After she wiped her face, "I saw a woman die on camera last night!"

Janice rushed over and silenced her by putting her hand over her mouth.

"Don't you say another word." She leaned toward her ear and whispered, "We have to find someplace else to talk. These walls have ears."

Courtney didn't understand. She thought her home was the perfect place to have privacy.

"Why can't we talk here?"

Janice grabs her purse. "Let's walk."

They took a walk down the street to talk. Janice points out all the cameras on the poles. She also points out the cameras from Oxicure.

"Janice, I already know where all the cameras are located, I work for Oxicure!"

"Courtney, there is a lot that you don't know. Look up, do you see the reflection that keep zipping by throughout the day?"

"Yes, I do see that. I been seeing that since I was little. My friends and I use to pretend that it was aliens spying on us."

"They are not aliens; those are drones that conduct 24-hour surveillance. The Orders use them to monitor our lives without our permission or consent. The last thing that you least expect is the phone that's in your hand."

Courtney is shocked, "What, you got to be joking, my phone!"

"When have I ever joked with you like this? Before you were born, phones were handheld."

Courtney thought that was hilarious, "Handheld, what! You are telling me that old people had to carry a phone around everywhere with them?"

Janice replied, "Um, yes. The phones then would transmit a signal through satellites."

Courtney was blown away by this history lesson, "What will you tell me next, you had to type into the phone to send a message?"

Janice replied," Yes, but that's not the point. The point I'm trying to make is that the Order began to violate its own people's rights. Their phones had tracking devices created in them. The Orders upgraded and had access to your messages, pictures, videos, and everything. If a crime was committed, they accessed your location to see were you in the vicinity. They were making convictions while violating your rights at the same time. Now your rights are not being violated. When your pain free phone was installed, you signed over all your rights for the Orders access. The reason the phone is under the skin has nothing to do with convenience Courtney. The Order has connected that phone to your central nervous system. Have you seen that new 007 movie with Pamela Stone as 007?"

Courtney thought about it for minute, "Is that the movie where 007 got all the fems?"

"Yes. Have you noticed that they always use a lie detector test to see if your lying? That's the same way your phone is connected."

It's becoming reality to Courtney, "Shit. That's why Brandy always asking about my heart rate and everything, it's through my phone! Why are you telling me this now?"

Janice asked her, "Do you still have the note I gave you earlier?"

She pulls it out of her pocket. "Put your phone against it and call Lacey."

Courtney looking confused, "I can't. It has to be against glass or something."

Janice explains, "It's like electricity and copper, as long as it has a conductor, electricity can travel through it. Electricity can't travel through objects like rubber because it's identified as a dead object. That note I wrote to you is on a dead object. None of the Orders systems can read it. The same with the hand gestures. It is called Jaz language from the old world."

Courtney is trying to process it all.

She grabbed the cardboard and her parent eye liner and wrote, "How do you remember stuff from the old world?"

Janice wrote and signed, "I have to explain it to you later."

Courtney shook her head, "Okay."

Courtney phone starts ringing. She saw that it was Vanessa, "We have to go back to the house."

"Why," Janice replied.

"I forgot that Vanessa supposed to meet me at the house. She on that case I was trying to tell you about."

She answers the phone, "Vanessa, give me a minute, I'm almost home."

### 

Bria and her team just made it back to the compound. It is a mess. Stuff was everywhere. Their hearts dropped when they saw what happened. Several women tended to one of the Elders that was pushed down. Elder Anna was laying on the floor covered up with a sheet. Bria dropped her backpack and ran to Lisa's room to check on her. As she got closer to her room, she saw drops of blood that led to the entrance of Lisa's door. Bria breathing became short, her imagination caused her to have a panic attack. She was thinking that her sibling was dead. After getting control of her breathing she rushed in the room. Lisa was sitting on her pallet bloody. The gun and the knife were on the bed next to her.

   Bria looked at her sibling, "Are you okay?"

   Lisa replied with tears, "I couldn't save Elder Anna, I couldn't save her!"

   Bria ran over and hugged her tight, "It's okay Lisa, you did good. You hear me, you did good. I'm sorry I left you. I don't want to ever leave you again!"

Bria and the other three fems took the lead. They appointed others to get the place cleaned as they gathered all the info they needed. The bodies of the ones Lisa killed was put in a death wrap. These wraps were made from very flammable recycled material. They were created for cremations. There was an old funeral home that wasn't far from the entrance of the subway. It was on the edge of the Outwards. When the residents of the Outwards saw the towering red light on, they paid their respects for the lost by flashing their house lights off and on. Bria instructed 12 fems to cremate the bodies while the Elders prepared the body of Elder Anna. They dressed her in what they called a Holy Suit. It was a quilted robe that was made with pieces of garments that the Elders that died before her wore. She wasn't taken immediately to be buried. It was customary that the deceased had to sleep at least one night, or the Elders job was not complete on this side of life. They had to wait until morning.

Those that left with Bria earlier stayed and talked to Lisa. She explained to them what happened.

"I was watching my show when I heard a loud scream. Sometimes when the younger fems playing, they scream and holler but this scream was different. I peeked around the corner, and I saw the Web destroying our stuff. I was pissed. They were breaking our stuff and throwing our things like it was trash. The fems from the Remnant did absolutely nothing. They just stood there and let them do what they wanted to do. Elder Anna is the only one that stood up to their leader."

Bria interrupted, "How did the leader look and have you seen her before?"

Lisa told her that she never seen her before," She was really tall and had a lot of muscles but Elder wasn't afraid of her."

She became emotional, "When Elder Anna didn't listen to her, their leader became angry. That's when she took her cane and started beating her." My heart sank when I saw Elder Anna laying there bleeding and all the fems we have here just stood and watched."

Tiffany said, "We left Kayla and Julian in charge, what did they do?"

Lisa replied, "They hid. When I ran to the back looking for a weapon, I saw both of them hiding in the closet in the Elders room."

Tonya got angry "See, that's bullshit I been talking about. This the shit we been taught all our lives, run, and hide. How long we going to keep taking loss and losing lives? They were in the closet hiding like some cowards!"

Bria tried to calm her, "It's okay Tonya."

"Bria, shut the fuck up. It's not alright. I'm tired of you always trying to be the voice of damn reason. What would have happened if your sibling didn't find that gun and the knife? What if Web would have found it first? It would have been a damn massacre. We already lost one elder; we have to do something different!"

Lisa said, "I agree, we have to do something different. Let's teach them to fight back instead of expecting them to. I know how to fight but that was my first time using a gun on somebody. We can teach them to fight and how to use weapons to defend the compound. Can I say something and it can't leave this room?"

They all agreed that whatever she said wouldn't leave the room, "I know this sound strange, but when I pulled that trigger and stabbed that fem with that blade, it actually felt good".

Teja agreed.

### 

Courtney needed to clear her mind. Her thoughts were running rapid. She decided to go with Vanessa back to her place. Vanessa asked her not to say anything until they got to her place. After arriving at her apartment, Courtney noticed that she didn't have any cameras. There was no electronics at all. This was different. Only the Outwards went without electronics devices but at least they had PVs to watch. Vanessa worked as a police officer but lived totally off the grid. As soon as she entered her home, she made Courtney put on a glove over her phone to kill the signal. Vanessa tested it by using her phone to call. When it came back that her phone was offline, she covered her phone also.

"Okay Courtney we can talk freely without being monitored."

Courtney was intrigued, "Where did you learn all this stuff from?"

"My parent. She taught me all this when I was younger. She also taught me about Jaz language."

Courtney started laughing.

Vanessa said, "What's funny?"

"My parent just told me about that today. I watched her do these hand gestures all my life and I had no clue where it came from, until today."

Vanessa explained to her how the language came about.

"Back in the old days, there was a fem named Jaz that was deaf. One of her parents was a monster. It walked and talked like fems, but it was very mean and hurt her a lot. Her other parent died while giving birth to her sibling."

Courtney was confused, "Hold up, wait a minute. I didn't say nothing when you said her other parent was a monster, I just went along with it. I know we learned that shit in school when they talked about myths of old, but you totally lost me when you said her parent gave birth to the sibling. Give birth? Birth is given at Fertilicom. It has always been, you go to Fertilicom, pick out the avatar you like, wait for I think about 7 months or so, pay market value and pick up the baby."

Vanessa tried to explain it better, but it was hard for Courtney to erase what she has been programmed to believe.

"Okay, lets skip the part about birth and the monster part. They said that Jaz killed herself and her sibling grew up and taught other fems to communicate through her language. To fast forward, this is one of the only languages that went undetected in the new world of Femdom. None of our systems can interpret it."

"How did your parent get the stamp and still remembered these stories from the old world? All the old fems had to get a mental cleansing and that was to wipe their minds free from the lies of religion and all the things that hurt you. You have to make this shit make sense cause all this sound like, is bullshit Vanessa."

Vanessa was being very patient with Courtney in her ignorance.

"During the time of the mind cleanse, some got the stamp without going through the three treatments. Remember, it's not about what you know, it's who you know. You really think that the rich, wealthy and the very elite of Femdom had to go through the cleanse and get a stamp? That's why the law was created that if you talk about the Undiscussed, or somehow have literature or books from the old world, you will go to prison and can even be put to death", Vanessa explained.

Courtney sarcastically said, "Oh they can be put to death, okay, this is a little too much. In 22 years of living. I have never known anyone to be put to death for knowing or talking about the old world, have you?"

"Yeah, my parent!" the room went silent.

Courtney was speechless.

"When I was 10 yrs. old, my parent was caught communicating with an Outwards that she was friends with from the old world. She had no idea that her phone calls were recorded and used against her. The worse part about it is, Oxicure was responsible for her demise. They reported her to the Orders."

Courtney became anxious," I have to go. This is too much for real. I thought we was here to talk about the fem you found earlier. I just wanted to see if it was the same fem I catch the train with."

Vanessa apologized, "I'm sorry for throwing all this info on you at one time. I wanted us to talk somewhere safe. I hope all this won't interfere with us being friends."

Courtney replied, "It's not. I just have to go and get some sleep. My brain is tired after hearing all this shit."

Vanessa was understanding. She was about to remove their gloves until she thought about something.

"Wait, before you leave, can you look at the picture of the fem we found today?"

Vanessa grabbed the pictures from an offline E-file she stored it in. Courtney confirmed by the dress and shoes that it's the same fem that was at the judge's home in Zone 8. Just as she was about to close down the file, Courtney asked her to go to another picture. She thought she saw a picture with a name tattooed on her back. When Vanessa enlarged the photo, it revealed her name and it was Azavia. Courtney took her glove off and ran out the house. As soon as she arrived at the train station, she received a phone call from Lacey.

"Where you been? I been calling your phone and it was doing some weird 2055 shit?"

Courtney wasn't really in the mood to talk, "I was out talking to a friend I met at the club the other day. Where you at?"

"I'm out around the city riding with Shae. She a prospect I been talking to for a few weeks." Courtney train just arrived, "Call me when you make it home Lacey".

Lacey hung up the phone with Courtney. Shae asked, "Is your friend ok?"

"Yeah, she good. I just get worried about her whenever I call her and she don't answer. I look at her like she's my younger sibling."

Shae was impressed, "Look at you. Trying to take care of someone other than yourself."

"Shit, I'm not selfish, especially when it comes to my friends. So where exactly are we going?"

Shae jokingly said, "If I tell you, I have to kill you".

Lacey laughed it off.

"I told you my parent having a big party tonight. All her rich friends supposed to be there. Her parties are really big."

Lacey was excited. Shae remembered one of the singers that supposed to host it.

"Have you ever heard of Shante,' the R&B singer?"

Lacey replied with excitement, "Yes, I love her music. My favorite song is Petrified!"

"You are joking, I love that song too." She told her car to play the song and they rode around till about 10pm.

Shae's parent home is like something off of PV. The driveway to get from the street to her front door seemed like a mile. It was beautiful. Lacey took pictures of the house with her lenses. She wanted to show off, so she sent the pics to Courtney phone. Lacey had no idea that this was a red carpeted event. One of the most popular movie producers, Alex K., was even there. She created movies about super sheroes and was known all around the world of Femdom. Lacey felt like royalty when they pulled up in front of the red carpet. The lights from the paparazzi lit up the entrance. The music could be heard outside. They got out the car and was greeted by some of the guest. Shae was familiar with this type of attention and parties, but Lacey was acting like a kid at a candy store. Shae grabbed her hand and walked through the grand doors of the house.

They were greeted with drinks from one of the many servers.

Lacey was still in awe, "Shae, you didn't tell me it was this type of party."

She asked her, "What do you mean, this type of party?"

"The type of parties where you have famous people. Look, that's the fem off that new show, 'The Outward Renegade!'

The deeper they got in the house the more celebrities appeared.

Shae said, "I'm going to find my parent so just hang out for a little bit and I will be right back."

As soon as Shae walked off, several fems approached Lacey. Shae went in search of her parent. She noticed that one of her parent guards was standing at the door to her office.

She walked to the door and looked at the guard.

"Who are you staring at?"

The guard replied, "Can I help you, Shae?"

Shae said to her, "You sound like a damn identITy profile, can I help you looking ass. Get out my way."

She put her arm across the French doors leading to her office, "Look Shae, this shit not personal like you always take it. Your parent has company. She instructed me not to let anyone in. Anyone includes you."

Shae agreed and acted like she was walking away. The guard dropped her arm and Shae twisted the knob and entered the office. When she walked in, she saw Judge Camilla handing her parent a stack of money. She jumped up from the couch.

"Fem Madam, I told her not to enter but you know she don't listen," the guard replied.

Madam consoled her, "It's okay Natasha. Hey babe."

Camilla walked over to Shae and hugged her.

"How are you, Shae? Long time no see. What have you been up too?"

Shae put her head down, "I been ok Judge. It has been a while. Almost 3 years."

Camilla started to cry.

"I'm so sorry for bringing that up Judge."

"It's okay, I just can't believe they killed my baby. It doesn't even seem like three years. All these cameras and nobody saw what happened to my child. I wanted to burn down every piece of shit house in the Outwards to find out who did it."

She saw that Shae started feeling down.

"I know that you two were best friends and you miss her as much as I do. It will be okay."

Shae put her head down. The Judge lifted her chin up.

"Look at me. Time does make things better."

She turned towards Madam, "I'm about to go to the party and see who I see. Natasha, can you walk me down?" Natasha agreed.

"What's going on Madam?" Her parent grabbed her hand and pulled her close enough to get a hug.

"Where have you been? I been calling you and you haven't returned any of my calls. I be worrying about you Shae."

Shae sat on the couch, "I have been really preoccupied with this prospect I met. Her name is Lacey. I really like her Madam. I don't need you trying to interrogate her either."

"Lacey, I don't know any Lacey's. Who are her parents?"

"I don't know all of that yet Madam, but if you want to meet her, she is downstairs on the dancefloor waiting on me."

Fem Madam told her that she will meet her downstairs in a little bit. Shae walked out and Natasha walked in and closed the door.

"You wanted to speak to me Madam?"

Madam was pacing the floor, "I need to speak to you and your partner in crime, Lashawn, where is she?"

Natasha is getting nervous, "She was right behind me!"

As she spoke, Lashawn casually walked in with a plate of finger foods, "Theses little sandwiches are delicious."

Madam fuse was ignited. She grabbed a ceramic bowl that sat upon the table next to the couch and threw it at her. She ducked, the bowl hit the door behind her.

Madam asked, "Why did you two dumb asses throw the young girl's body in the trash around the corner from the fucking judges house? I told you two idiots to get rid of the fem. You could have driven her back to the Outwards and dumped her body anywhere. That place is a giant cemetery with no headstones but no, you had to be lazy. Now the police are involved."

Natasha attempted to apologize, "I'm sorry Madam. How can we fix this shit?"

Madam was looking for something to throw again, "Fix, what you mean fix? Oxicure already have that night stored in its memory. You two need to go there and get that entire day's video and audio and destroy it. The judge paid me to make sure her name won't come up. If her name come up, they will probably start investigating what really happened to her daughter. All they have to do is trace it back to me and I'm ruined. So, find a way to fix it before I pay you two to kill each other!"

Before they left the room, Madam asked a question, "I heard someone went and killed one of the Remnant elders. I also heard it was someone with a Web tattoo on her hand. I don't ever want to find out which one of you, heartless pieces of shit, did that. Elder Anna was like a sibling to me. Take that secret to your grave! Now get the fuck out of my office!"

Lacey and Shae is having a drink and socializing. Fem Madam has calmed down and is headed down the stairs to interact more with her guests. Shae excuses herself and grabs her parent hand so she could introduce her to Lacey.

"Lacey this is my parent, everyone calls her Madam and Madam, this is Lacey."

# 4

This is a morning of mourning for the Remnant. They are preparing to deliver her soul back to the Creator. Elder Anna was one of the oldest elders that remained. She was the backbone that held the tradition of the Remnant together for their sect. There was no distinct direction with her absence. The subways were silent as the entire eastern sect of Remnant assembled.

Back in the Inwards, Fem Madam spent this morning differently. She had an all-black dress made, along with a black veil that matched. She is routinely awakened on Saturday morning by her chef with breakfast. Today she chose to fast, she was grieving. After she had gotten dressed, Natasha asked her if she needed a ride anywhere.

"I do need a ride, call Sam from Twilight to meet me here in 30 minutes."

Natasha didn't know how to feel about that. A thousand thoughts went through her mind. She always drove Madam everywhere she needed to go, what made today so different.

"Fem Madam, I can take you where you need to go, you don't need to call Sam!"

Madam replied, "Natasha, where I need to go, I don't think that you will be welcomed."

Natasha looking confused, "But I always go everywhere with you. What make today different."

Madam ignores her and continue to get ready to go. "I'm not doing anything this morning Madam so I can take you!"

Madam whispers as she fix her veil in the mirror.

"How are you going to take me to see someone that you maliciously murdered?"

Her voice starts to escalate, "I heard you killed my friend because she wouldn't listen to you. That's the dumbest shit I ever heard of. You must have forgotten where you come from you gutter piece of shit. I saved you from the same low life's you run with now. The Outwards sold you to me for a loaf of bread and a pack of lunch meat. Your parents were dropheads. They died from overdosing on eyedrop drugs. I didn't even let the Outwards get their paws on you because I saw power and strength in you."

Natasha became emotional. "I have given you a damn good life, why would you run around with the scum of New Daphne?"

Natasha is feeling bad. Madam made her feel lower than low.

"I run with them so I can feel a sense of family. I have no family! You have no idea how it feel to be sacrificed for drugs. I was a little fem and I have been with more fems by the time I was 7 than most adult fems have in a lifetime. I knew whenever anyone talked to me, held me, looked at me, it was for sex. When I became part of the Web, I noticed that they didn't want nothing from me. Most of them had no family just like me."

Madame asked her, "Why did you kill her, why did you kill my friend?"

Natasha started laughing, "You really want to know why?"

Madam turned toward her, "That's the least that you can do."

"I killed Anna because she reminded me of my parent. No one could tell her shit. She lived as though she did no wrong in that religious delusion, she called her view. I wasn't going to do anything to her at first but how can you disrespect me in front of the Web? That's my family, they respect and look up to me. I told her to sit down and be quiet. she ignored me in front of my fems. She knew who I was, and she still didn't give me any damn respect!"

Madam became agitated, "You were in someone else's home demanding for some respect? How dare you!"

The tension is swelling like yeast. Natasha starts to cry.

"See, that's what I mean. She is dead and she still couldn't do no wrong!"

Fem Madam slaps her twice, "Now that's enough. You haven't lived long enough to count her sins or her good deeds."

"Her sins? She taunted me Madam. She winked at me and started singing that song you use to sing all the time:' To God be the glory, to God be the glory, forever and forevermore', so I hit her until she stopped. If she was such a good person, how can you have a kid and act like they don't exist. She threw her away like fucking trash and everyone looking to her like she some kind of saint."

Madam got angry, "Don't you bring my child in this, and she didn't throw Shae away, she gave her away?"

Natasha interrupted her, "Oh, just like my parents. How can you fix your lips to say she wasn't thrown away? Just because she didn't land in slop doesn't disrepute the fact that she was still tossed in the trash."

Madam stands face to face with Natasha, "Let me tell you something, if you ever tell Shae that Elder Anna was her parent, I will kill you myself. You have no idea the circumstances surrounding why she gave Shae to me. That's a secret that I will take to my grave. Do you understand me?"

Natasha slowly took a couple steps back, "I understand."

Madam grabbed her purse and pat dried her tears with a cloth, "Now I need you to call Sam and tell her to come meet me here in 10 minutes."

Natasha turned around, stepped out Madam's room and called Sam.

### 

The other Elders have prepared Anna's body for burial. There were no cemeteries in the Outwards. The rich in Femdom was globally buried and the poor was burned. Since so many religions made up the Remnant, their burial rights were still honored. Land was designated in every large city to fulfil their rights. An elder would pick out the six strongest fems to carry the body. She chose, Bria, Lisa and the three T's. It was an honor to them because of the respect that they had for Elder Anna.

When young fems were left without parents, Anna would take them in. Bria and Lisa's parents were not part of the Remnant, they were dropheads. These drops were so powerful that those that were addicted to it would sell whatever they could in order to get a refill. Because the

Outwards are poor, there was nothing to sale but themselves. Once they became undesirable, they would traffic their own kids.

Elder Anna found them in the Shadows hungry and impoverished. She took them in but located their parents. Because the Outwards are unpoliced, all matters are dealt with civilly. When she met with their parents they came to an agreement. Her parents put a monetary price on both of them.  They agreed that if she pay the asking price that they will give all rights to the Remnant. Anna agreed. It only took her two days to get the money. The siblings were now a part of the Remnant. Their parents wasn't heard of until a year later.

One evening Bria and Lisa played at the edge of the tracks. There were a few more fems playing with them. Their parents came and abducted them. When word got back to the elders about what happened, she immediately put together a team to get them. Tiffany and Teja mother, whose name was Bonnie, Natalie, and Shannon, left the compound with Anna. When they got to their home, one of the parents was on the couch sleep. They looked through the kitchen window and saw their other parent placing drops in her eyes. Their concern grew because they walked around the house and looked through all the windows that wasn't boarded and there was no sign of the siblings. Bonnie heard crying from the house next door. Her and two other fems went over to investigate. It was

Lisa and Bria. Two fems were in the bedroom with Bria and one was trying to undress Lisa on the couch.

Bonnie looked at Elder Anna and it was something about the way Anna shook her head, that gave her the ok. Bonnie took a knife out her pocket and quietly opened the door. Lisa cried as the fem pulled her shirt over her head. Bonnie grabbed Lisa hand and told her to run to the porch.

The fem tried to explain what was going on.

"Wait I was getting her cleaned up for a sleepover. I wasn't doing anything to hurt her!"

Lisa ran to the porch and into the arms of Natalie. Bonnie grabbed the fem that grabbed Lisa and placed her in a choke hold.

She whispered in her ear, "Where is Bria?"

The fem started stuttering, "We wasn't going to hurt them."

Bonnie lifted her underarm and slid the blade of her knife into her lung as she gasped for air. Bonnie left her on the couch as she peeked into the only bedroom in the house. She saw a fem having sex with Bria and another sitting on the bed taking drops. She pushed the door open and punched the fem that was on top of Bria. Bonnie grabbed her hand and told her to get dressed and run to Natalie, who was waiting on the porch. While she put her clothes on the fem she hit tried to explain.

"We paid for both of them. Their parents sold them to us."

The one that was putting drops in her eye didn't say a word. She was spaced out because of the drugs. As soon as she heard Bria's little sandals on the porch, Bonnie closed the door to the room. She punched the woman talking until she was tired. The entire time the other fem stared at the ceiling. As the blooded fem begged for her life.

Bonnie placed her forearm under her neck, "You don't deserve to live, so you will die without mercy."

She slowly eased the knife in her heart. With one small twist, she cut her lights out. She stood to her feet and looked at the other fem. The sad part was that she was still dazed off looking at the ceiling as if nothing took place. Bonnie shook her head in disgust. With one swipe, she sliced her neck. She fell back on the bed with her eyes still gazing at the ceiling.

Natalie and LaShawn walked Bria and her sibling next door. As soon as they stepped in the driveway, they both began to cry. They didn't want to go back to their parents' house. Elder Anna stepped out the shadow on side the house to comfort the fems.

"Listen, you will never have to come back to this house again, you hear me?"

Bonnie closed the door to the neighbor's house. She saw them standing in the driveway of Lisa and Bria's house. As soon as she walked over to them, Anna told Bonnie and Shannon to take the sibling's back to the compound.

  Bonnie asked, "You sure, you don't need me to stay?"

  She reassured her, "Everything will be ok. Get them home and cleaned up. We won't be too far behind you."

Elder Anna let them get a good distance away before they entered the home of their parents. Anna pulled out a long dagger and Natalie pulled out a bat like club. Natalie kicked the door open and started wailing on the first parent with the club. The first hit knocked her to the floor. She stood over her and hit her in the head until her brains were exposed. The other parent walked out the bathroom as if she was floating on a cloud.

  When Elder Anna shoved the dagger in her windpipe she told her, "Look at me, you will no longer be able to hurt those children. They will be safe with me."

  She looked at Elder Anna, "Thank you!" She released a single tear, before she died.

All these things are going through their minds as they carry her to her final spot of rest. Normally there is no public interaction between the Outwards and the Remnant but today is different. A lot of the Outwards lined the streets as she was carried to the hilltop. Tears fogged their vision as they walked through the streets of the Outwards. The Remnant was shocked that so many people loved and respected Anna. They got to the hilltop and set her bed on a table that was prepared for her. Each of the remaining Elders had a chance to have words before she was laid to rest.

While the last elder spoke, a really expensive black car pulled up. Everyone was in awe. There were no cars like this in the Outwards. The driver exited the car. She walked to the other side and opened the door; it was Fem Madam. You could hear a pin drop at that moment. Madam put her shades on, and walked toward the area that the elders were speaking from. Some kids from the Outwards ran over by the car.

One fem was about to touch the door and the driver said, "Get your bad asses away from Fem Madam car!"

They were afraid and took off running. The Elders gave space to Fem Madam and allowed her to speak:

"Good morning. A lot of you know me as Fem Madam but my Order name that was given to me from birth is JoAnn. I have a few words to say about Elder Anna. Anna was a friend of mine. Let me take that back, we were more like siblings. My parent and her parent were siblings. I remember what we use to call it back then; the good ole days. There was a time when there wasn't anything called Outwards and Inwards. We were one and we called each other family. The most prized possession during that time was the family. There was no Remnant, no Web, none of those things. We actually spent time together learning about God and how to work together as a society. Now all that has changed. One person that I can say never changed with the times is Elder Anna. Believe it or not, growing up, I was the nice one and Anna was the mean one. She was mean in a good way though. She hated bullies and wouldn't let anyone pick on JoAnn.

After the Remnant was created, she dedicated her life for good. Her heart was for helping young fems.

Madam started to get emotional.

"I just want to take this time to say to her, thank you. Thank you for always being there for me and also giving me the best gift imaginable. As you enter your final resting place today, I want you to know that I love you and I will continue doing what I promised you I would."

Madam kneeled down and grabbed a handful of dirt, she walked over to her body and sprinkled the dirt on her hands:

"Ashes to ashes, dust to dust."

She took her shades off and sung a piece of the song they use to sing together," To God be the glory, to God be the glory, forever and forevermore.'

She walked to her car. There wasn't a dry face at the burial ground. Sam opened the back door for her.

When they were about to leave, Madam told her, "Bring me home. I'm not in the mood to go to the Twilight right now. Once you drop me off, I need you to go to Tanya's market and have them to cater food for 100 guest and drop it off at the Remnants compound. Bring someone with you because it can be dangerous down here but do not bring NaTasha here, ever again!"

### 

While the ceremony continued, Courtney tossed and turned in her bed late that morning. She wrestled to awake from her dream to no avail. She found herself in the Outwards again. This time she walked from house to house knocking on each door. The last house, she stepped on the porch and knocked on the door. The door opened and it was an elevator. When she went into the elevator, the door closed immediately behind her. She turned and there was only one button to push, down. The elevator seemed like it was going down 100 stories fast. Courtney gripped the handrail in the elevator so tight that it left an indention on it. The elevator stopped and the lights went out. The doors opened and Courtney peeked her head out before she stepped out. It look like the door opened to a hospital baby ward. There were incubators stacked in storage. She walked cautiously down the dark hall. Her footsteps activated the lights. A nurse walked up to her and asked do she need any help.

Courtney asked her, "Can you tell me where I am?"

The nurse replied, "You have to ask the right questions."

Courtney looked her badge and the name on it was Zia Moore. She heard the thunderous voice of the monster again calling her name. She turned in the direction of the voice and she was back outside in the Outwards.

She woke up to the voice of Brandy again, "Your heart rate is spiking, do you need medical attention?"

Courtney is at the end of her rope with Brandy.

"No, I don't need any medical attention. What I need to know is, why do I keep having these dreams?"

Brandy replied, "I cannot answer that question for you."

"Damn, what question can you answer," Courtney said in frustration.

"I can answer the question you may have about the nurse in your dream."

Courtney is dumbfounded, "How the fuck do you know about my dreams, this the first time I had a nurse in my dreams?"

"Brandy replied, "I am not allowed to answer that question."

Courtney became irate, she grabbed her light on the nightstand and threw it against the wall, "WHY CAN'T YOU ANSWER MY QUESTIONS?"

"I am a security device. Some information I am not programmed to give because it violates my systems security codes."

Courtney is now pacing the floor, trying to remember the details of the dream as she talked to herself.

"Okay, I got off the elevator and there were a lot of those baby machines……the nurse. What was that nurse name?"

Brandy answered, "The nurse in your dream name is Zia Moore."

"Shit, okay, is Zia Moore a real person", Courtney asked?

"Zia Moore is a real person."

Courtney went around the house looking for something to write on. She found a box and wrote on it with some eye liner.

"Brandy, tell me about Zia Moore," Courtney asked.

"Dr. Zia Moore was an American scientist. Her last known place of employment was with Fertilicom. Dr. Zia Moore created a virus called Chromovirus."

Courtney was excited to finally get some info about her dream.

"What is Chromovirus?"

Brandy went into alert mode. Some words, conversations and topics create alerts. These alerts are sent to Oxicure.

"I cannot answer any questions about that."

"Okay Brandy, where is Zia Moore now?" Courtney replied.

Brandy was still in secure mode, "I cannot answer any of your questions."

Courtney was angry, "Fuck you Brandy, I will find out on my own."

Because the alert was sounded at Oxicure, one of the employees responded to Courtney while she was getting dressed.

"Hello, we received an alert, are you okay? Do anyone at your address need medical attention?

Courtney waves at the camera, "No I am fine, I just probably need a system upgrade because mine is getting old and stupid."

"Oxicure will disarm the alert, have a good day."

Courtney delightfully said, "You too!"

Courtney finished getting dressed and grabbed a bag and put some lunch in it. She grabbed the box with the writing on it and rushed toward the door. She twisted the handle but couldn't open the door.

"Brandy, unlock the door."

Brandy replied," I cannot unlock the door at this time. I was created for your security. I am detecting that you are going to search for the doctor in your dream."

Courtney was nervous, she has never been locked in her own home, "I am not going to look for anyone in my dreams, it's just a dream."

Brandy replied," You are lying".

She is becoming angry, "This is my house, open the door Brandy!"

Brandy replied again, "No".

Courtney tried the back door, there was no way out. She has become a prisoner in her own home. She decided to try to start a fire on the stove. In case of fires, the doors are automatically unlocked. She placed a piece of meat on a skillet and turned the electric eye on as high as it went. As the meat start to burn Brandy alerted Courtney.

"The meats temperature is too hot. I cut the burner off to avoid risk of a fire."

Courtney screamed, "Brandy, let me out this house!"

Brandy asked," Do you need medical attention? I noticed your heart rate is rising?"

"Yes, yes, I need medical attention now," Courtney said as she laid on the floor by the front door.

Oxicure was alerted and they sent out medical assistance. When the two assistants knocked at the door and identified themselves, Brandy shut off the alert and disengaged all the locks. When the door opened Courtney grabbed her things and ran out the house.

# 5

It is 2pm. Janice had to work the second shift for her friend. Her friend normally worked the 6th floor but the supervisor sent her to the 12th floor for the day. Janice got her cart together and all her cleaning supplies and went to work. So many fems overlooked the complexity of housekeeping. If cleaning up behind fems is not hard enough, think about getting hit on in almost every room.

Whenever housekeeping come to clean a room, their routine was to knock first. If there is no answer or no instructions on the door, their key code would disarm the alarm system. Part of each tenant's rental agreement was to have a security system installed and active. When the tenants were up to no good, they would learn their workers routine. When it was time to clean their room, they would either lay in bed naked or they pretended to be coming out the shower when housekeeping is cleaning in order to seduce them into sex. Janice has been doing housekeeping for so long, she learned to work around these types of advances.

While she began her shift, Natasha and Lashawn met for lunch. Lashawn had no clue why they were meeting without Fem Madam. They sat in a secured booth. Most restaurants had security systems setup for the owners and employee's protection. Some created secured sections for customers that wanted to have private conversations. This conversation between them will be private.

They ordered two alcoholic beverages and a lunch special.

Lashawn looked around, "What's going on? We never meet here without Madam?"

"Madam couldn't make it for lunch today. She is in the Outwards for a funeral."

Lashawn was confused, "Funerals aren't allowed in the Outwards, what are you talking about."

"Funerals are permitted in the Outwards for certain people. The Orders allow Remnant members to be buried. They don't do the poor fem cremations."

Lashawn had no clue, "What make them so special?"

Natasha responded with a little animosity, "They are fems just like us. They eat, shit, and die just like us. The only thing that set us apart is what they make people believe about them. They walk around like they have some special word from God. Have you ever listened to the junk they talk about?"

"No, I haven't," she replied.

"You not missing shit. I grew up around the Remnant and they proved to be weak and fearful. They preach that their God did not give them a spirit of fear but every time you see them, they are doing what, hiding. Do you know how contradicting that shit is?

Lashawn said, "I thought they hid underground?"

"They do, that's what I'm saying. They live in fear underground. Even when you see one of them outside the tunnels, they are hiding their faces with those goofy ass outfits."

Lashawn became inquisitive," How did Madam know the person that died?"

"They were like siblings. I been knowing her my entire life. Her name was Anna. She was one of the Elders that supposed to have dedicated her life to protecting the kids in the Outwards. I hated her and she knew it."

The food they ordered was hot and ready. They started to eat.

Lashawn continued the conversation, "I never heard of an elder name Anna in the Outwards. Probably because I grew up on the southside of New Daphne. What did she do to you that made you feel the way you feel? It had to be fucked up cause hate is a strong ass word."

"She gave me back to my parents one time to many."

"Who, Madam or we still talking about the Anna lady?" Lashawn replied.

"Yeah, I'm still talking about Anna. My parents were a part of Remnant at one time. They faithfully followed their teachings and beliefs until one of my parents became addicted to those damn drops and that was it. It didn't take long for my other parent to fall into the grip of that monster. They would pray over them and believe that somehow their God would get them off drugs, it didn't work. They would leave me days at a time with Elder Anna. She warned them about leaving me. If they did it again, she was going to bring me to their house in the Outwards and drop me off. Guess what?"

LaShawn shrugged her shoulders, "Shit, I don't know, she dropped you off?"

"Yes, she dropped me off. That was like a death sentence to me. No one to fight for my safety, or my wellbeing. What did she think was going to happen by leaving me with dropheads? They let all these nasty fems have sex with me!"

Lashawn almost choked on her food, "Oh shit, so you mad cause Anna didn't come back for you?"

Natasha replied, "No, I was mad because she left me. By the time she so called rescued me from my parents it was too fucking late. The damage was already done. Why would you leave me with two dropheads? The one thing I totally hated the most, was that stupid song they sung all the way back to the compound. That shit stuck in my head."

LaShawn replied," Damn, I'm sorry to hear about all that shit that happened to you. I don't want you to think that I don't care about what happened to you cause I really do. Me and you have been like siblings since Madam put me on the team. I'm not trying to change the subject but how long do these types of funerals last and why you brought me her to talk?"

"I don't know how long funerals last, shit, I never been to one," they start laughing.

"I spoke with Madam this morning before she left. She said that we have to fix that shit that we fucked up a couple days ago."

LaShawn attempted to check Natasha, "What you mean we, I told you that we could drop her off on the outside of the gate. She would have been with the Outwards and we could have moved on to the next job."

"What are you talking about? When Madam told us to get rid of the judge's child, you said the same shit. Now we have her about to start a war with the Outwards for nothing."

Lashawn accepted responsibility," Okay that was my idea but where do we go from here? The police already found her body. I'm sure they not going to make a big deal out of it. Once they see she is not stamped, they will bring her to the crematory in the Outwards."

NaTasha replied, "That's not the issue. The issue is Oxicure has a video of everything we done."

Lashawn stood up and start making a scene, "You joking, how do we suppose to `get into their system? We are done, we going to prison."

Natasha said, "Sit your ass down. We are not going to prison. There is a way that we can get the video!"

Lashawn sat down and calmed her nerves, "How do we suppose to get the video from Oxicure? That shit tied into the same system as the Orders."

"Do you remember Roxie from Twilight?" Natasha replied.
Lashawn didn't remember her.

"Roxie was the customer that always requested fems that wanted three fems in one setting," She reminded her.

 "Yes, now I remember. She the one that requested me one time and I'm not even in the catalog."

Natasha explains her plan, "I have her address. Her fem that she in a Union with name is Rebecca, works at Oxicure as a supervisor."

LaShawn gets the plan and they leave the restaurant.

### 

Courtney refused to use her phone. Since she escaped her home, she hasn't made contact with anyone. She has become totally paranoid. Since she stepped outside she hasn't stopped looking for drones that she think the Orders sent. She arrived at Vanessa house and beat on the door as if someone was chasing her. Vanessa heard that it was Courtney, she opened the door and pulled her in.

Vanessa asked, "What's wrong with you?"

She made hand gestures about her hand covering. Once their hand was covered, Courtney broke down.

She started telling her what happened, "My fucking identITy called me a liar and locked me in my own home!"

Vanessa replied, "What?"

"Yes, you heard me right, she locked me in my own house. I had to ask for medical assistance to escape!"

Vanessa started laughing, "It's time for an upgrade if she locking you in your own shit."

"No, it started with another bad dream. This time I was underground in a hospital surrounded by a lot of baby incubators. I turned around and a nurse was standing in front of me with a name badge that said Zia Moore."

Vanessa replied, "Did you say Zia Moore, as in Dr. Zia Moore?"

"Yes, Dr. Zia Moore!"

Vanessa was very excited. She told Courtney to follow her. She looked around her apartment as if Vanessa was going to have someone jump out on her. When Courtney entered her bedroom, she literally got on her knees and looked under the bed. That is how paranoid she had become. She grabbed her hand and took her into the bedroom closet.

"Courtney, you have to promise to never tell anyone what I'm about to show you!"

Courtney was thinking, why is she trying to show me the clothes in her closet but she still shook her head.

Vanessa said, "No, don't shake your head, you have to promise me!"

"Okay, yes, I promise," Courtney replied.

Vanessa created a faux wall in her closet. Behind the wall was a small room with boxes stored to the ceiling. After digging through a few boxes, she found one with the name Zia Moore. Vanessa began to explain to her that Dr. Zia worked for Fertilicom and so did her parent.

"My parent started working with Fertilicom right before Zia created a virus to destroy the monsters."

Courtney asked her, "What was so bad about the monsters that everyone wanted them gone if they really worked side by side with fems?"

"Dr. Zia work proved that sickness and diseases came from them mixing with fems. Let me ask you a question, when have you ever been sick?"

Courtney stood there speechless. She was thinking to herself, never.

"Have you ever seen someone that couldn't walk from a birth defect or was blind?" Vanessa asked.

Courtney thought about it for a second, "No I haven't. Maybe it was good that she got rid of them then. If she cleansed Femdom of sickness and disease, she is a real-life Shero."

Vanessa continued to explain, "She created a virus..."

Courtney jumped in," Called Chromovirus!"

"Yes, how did you know that?"

"Brandy told me that before she went completely crazy and started locking all the door and putting the fire out."

"What fire? You didn't say anything about no fire!" Vanessa was in shock.

Courtney brushed it off, "I will tell you about it later. Now what were you saying about Chromovirus".

My parent said that Fertilicom took the virus and sold it all around the Femdom to get rid of all the monsters. Dr. Moore didn't approve of that and when she said something, they fired her. She went underground and wasn't heard of again."

"Why I'm dreaming about her then?"

Vanessa said, "I have no idea. I can't answer that question for you."

"Did your parent know where she went? If they worked with her and it look like you have some of her research, they don't know where she disappeared to?"

Vanessa replied, "I heard that she was in Daphne when she worked for Fertilicom. Rumor has it that the subway turns into a place called the Shadows. It goes deep beneath the city, but no one goes there. They said the souls of the monsters live there but no one has ever been there to confirm that."

Courtney took a deep breath, "I want to go?"

Vanessa couldn't believe what she was hearing.

"What did you just say?"

Courtney replied, "You heard me right; I want to go! I don't think these dreams will stop until I go."

Vanessa told her, "If you go, I'm going too. I have read through all these boxes and listened to all the story's my parent use to tell me, now I want to see for myself!"

### 

Natasha and Lashawn just pulled up to the Plaza. The Plaza is one of the city's largest luxury housing complexes. Most of the older secured buildings only had cameras in the elevators and housing units. Natasha didn't want to be seen on camera, so they had to take the stairs. They walked to the 6th floor, and they were tired.

Lashawn said, "Damn, what floor do they live on? This is some bullshit; we have to walk one hundred flights of stairs!"

Natasha was tired and breathing hard, "They on the 12th floor, we almost there. Just think of it as leg day at the gym."

"Leg day, I never work on my legs for this reason, it hurts."

Janice shift has started off fairly quiet. She has been cleaning rooms and hasn't ran into any sexual advances. It was her break time so he headed toward the elevator. Destiny made a connection. Janice was passing the same door Natasha and Lashawn were entering the 12th floor through.

She bumped into both of them, "Excuse me, I didn't mean to bump into you," Janice said humbly.

"No problem," Natasha replied.

LaShawn was done. Her legs were shaking. She needed to lay down and take a nap after that walk. Janice looked at them through the corner of her eyes. The way they looked around for the door numbers, she knew something wasn't right. One thing Natasha did know about the building was how the security system worked.

They needed Janice badge to disarm Roxie's' room security. They timed it perfectly. They waited till they saw her walking by and bumped her. Lashawn stole her badge from her pocket. As soon as the elevator door closed, they went to room #1216. This is the place where Roxie and Rebecca lived. NaTasha knocked on the door, "Housekeeping!"

Roxie was watching PV and Rebecca was in the shower.

Roxie cut the volume down on the PV, "Housekeeping already cleaned this room!"

Natasha swiped the badge and unlocked the door.

Roxie rushed to the door, "You already cleaned this room!"

NaTasha pushed the door open, grabbed Roxie by the neck and pushed her on the couch. She pulled a bag from her pocket and covered her hands. The bags stopped her phone from transmitting.

LaShawn asked, "Where is Rebecca?"

Roxie had no idea what was going on, "She taking a shower, what do you want? I don't owe Twilight or anybody any money!"

Natasha replied, "Shut up. This have nothing to do with Twilight nor owing anyone money."

Roxie was confused, "Natasha, what did I do? You know me. I mind my own business and stay out of everyone's way."

NaTasha lifted her by her shirt, "I told you to shut up, we here to speak to Rebecca."

As she spoke, Rebecca walked out naked with a large towel covering her hair, "Who was that at the door?"

She looked up and saw Natasha and Lashawn standing in their living room.

"What the fuck" ….

Lashawn quickly grabbed her arm, before she could run back in the bathroom. She threw her on the floor in front of Roxie. Rebecca took the towel off her head and covered up with it. Lashawn covered both her hands with the same type of bags that was placed on Roxie's hands.

Natasha went and sat on the couch next to her.

"Okay let me explain what's going on and also, let me explain what I need the both of you to do. If both of you understand what I just said, I need the both of you to shake your head, yes."

They both looked at each other and shook their head.

"Thursday night while you were at work Rebecca, an alarm went off in Zone 8, do you remember that?"

Rebecca was extremely nervous. Her hands were trembling, "No, I don't remember."

Lashawn stepped over Rebecca on the floor and slapped Roxie. When Rebecca saw that, her memory of that day at work came back to her.

"Yes, I remember. I had Courtney work that zone on Thursday, yes, I remember. Please don't hit her again. I will do whatever you want me too!"

Natasha replied, "I know you will. Now I need you to listen and listen good. I need you Rebecca, to go to work."

"Rebecca interrupted her, "I'm off!" She looked at her and she apologized.

"Like I was saying. I need you to go to work, pull up the records and video from that day and erase it."

Rebecca lifted her hand, asking permission to speak, "How do I suppose to do that, Oxicure system is connected to the Orders main drive?"

Natasha angrily replied, "Figure the shit out!"

Rebecca raised her hand again. Natasha grabbed the towel that was covering her, "If you raise your hand one more time, I will use this towel to choke your ass to death, do you hear me?"

Rebecca shook her head, yes.

"Rebecca you are smart. I have checked your record. This will not be the first-time erasing video."

Rebecca looked at Roxie. "I know you remember Roxie's run in with the drop head from the Outwards. Oh, you three had fun that night, licking, kissing, and fucking each other. If I recall correctly, you ordered her for your birthday. Let me see… yep, it was you that ordered the eyedrop package. Every last one of you were high. I'm guessing the alarm at Oxicure went off multiple times when she began screaming out the window or did it go off when she fell from the 8th floor balcony?"

Roxie spoke for her, "She will do it! Babe go and put some clothes on and erase the damn video so they can let us go."

Lashawn started smiling, "I like that submissive shit. You tell her what to do and she just do it. That is sexy as fuck."

Rebecca hurried and put some clothes on. Natasha gave Lashawn stringent instructions.

"Go with her and make sure she doesn't call anyone. She is to go in her office, show you the file from that day. Watch her erase all the footage from that day in Zone 8. When she finish, bring her back here and we will kill them both."

Lashawn was okay with everything but the killing them both part.

"Hold up, you didn't say anything about killing anyone!"

Natasha replied, "Look, we can't leave any loose ends untied. If you have a problem with it, go and explain it to Fem Madam and see what she says."

Lashawn agrees to the deal and take the covering off Rebecca hands. "Before I take these off of you, I have a few rules. Don't mention my name and make sure you tell me where the cameras are because I don't want to be seen."

### 

Vanessa loaded up two military size backpacks for her and Courtney. She put lights, food, knives and even had two small tents.

Courtney laughed at first and then she asked, "What do we need all this stuff for? We just going to the subway."

Vanessa reassured her, "We need this and even more stuff, The part where we are going is really deep beneath the city. Depending on what we encounter while we down there, it could take us a couple days or longer."

Courtney began to second guess herself, "This probably is a little too much to be asking of you and we just met."

Vanessa became emotional, "I have been waiting my entire life for an opportunity like this. My parent died with all these things in her. I just want to see if it was all real or did, she die for a fairy tale."

Courtney is trying to prepare herself mentally, "I need to tell my parent what I'm doing. Will I be able to use my phone down there?"

Vanessa grabs three guns and several clips.

"Once we are there, the phones will not be able to track us or anything. I understand that you have never been on the other side of the gate but if you just follow my lead, you will be safe."

She handed her a piece of paper to write on, "We will drop this off to your house on the way out."

"NOOO, Courtney screamed, Brandy locked me in the house. Something is seriously wrong with my identITy. I don't want to step another foot in that house!"

Vanessa told her," You don't have to step in the house. We can leave the note on the door where your mom can find it."

### 

Janice has spent all her lunch time looking for her badge. She had to get a temporary pass in order to finish her shift. She walked over to the elevator, and she saw Rebecca and Lashawn, breathing hard, coming out of the staircase. She assisted her by holding her arm as they walked out the building. Janice thought that was very suspicious.

She went back to the 12th floor and knocked on their door, "Hello housekeeping."

Natasha asked Roxie, "Why is housekeeping back?"

"I have no idea. Maybe she forgot something!"

Natasha grabbed her by the hair, "You better tell that fem to come back later or this will be her last day at work."

Roxie walked to the door, "You already been here today, Samantha, everything is clean. Can you lock the door back, I will see you tomorrow."

Janice swiped her card, locking the door, arming the system. All tenants in this building were taught during new resident orientation about what to do during an emergency. One of the universal codes that indicate that you are in trouble is, Samantha. Natasha knew, once she entered an apartment with housekeeping master key, the security is disarmed. That's why she used the key to enter the apartment. What she didn't know is when housekeeping leave and lock the door, it automatically set the alarm back to its default. Roxie and Rebecca kept their identITy on silent so whenever there is an emergency, the trespasser wouldn't know the alert was sounded.

When Janice heard it, she immediately knew what to do. She continued her shift but didn't go too far from their apartment. The alarm was set but not alerted.

Lashawn and Rebecca have arrived at Oxicure. It was a very secure building. Roxie had to get her in with a new hire visitors pass. The process is to take a copy of her ID and submit it to security. Rebecca knew the young fem at the front desk. She was young and didn't want to go through all the necessary steps. She just let them in. Lashawn attempted to avoid the cameras by walking with her head down. After navigating through the building, they finally made it to her office.

Rebecca explained to Lashawn, "Before we go in, I have to talk to the on-duty supervisor and let her know why I am in the building."

Lashawn didn't understand, "You don't have to tell her shit. Just go in there and do what you have to and we can get out of here."

Rebecca tries to reason with her, "Look, we have a strict protocol here. This is the largest security system in Femdom. China even uses Oxicure."

Lashawn is getting upset. She grabbed Rebecca by her shirt, "Look, I don't give a damn about Oxicure's world overview. You talking to me as if I'm trying to get a job here for real. Let's get in, erase the video, and get out of here! Remember, Natasha is at the house with your fem."

Rebecca opened the door and walked through the monitoring room with Lashawn. None of the employees paid any attention to them. Rebecca was extremely nervous. She rushed to her computer as soon as she entered her office. Lashawn instructed her to text Roxie and tell her that you are at the job. She texted Roxie and Natasha saw the text. Natasha needed to know they made it so she could know when to kill Roxie. Rebecca started to pull up all the alert data from the last week. While she worked, Lashawn watched the monitors.

Natasha started to pace the floor. She really didn't want to kill Roxie but she felt it was necessary. She stood in front of the PV and pulled a gun from her pocket.

Roxie was afraid, "What are you doing Natasha? We have done everything that you asked. You already know that we not going to tell shit!"

Her heart was racing. It was so bad that an alert was sent to Oxicure for med check. The fem that worked Zone 72 noticed the alert. She called for the on-duty supervisor, Georgette.

"We have an alert at Zone 72. The audio have been disabled but the video was sustained."

Georgette checked the cameras and saw Natasha standing in front of the couch with a gun in her hand.

"Since we don't have any audio, make sure you document everything you see!"

She ran to her office. With a silent alert, the police has to be contacted to do a wellness check. While Rebecca continued to work on erasing Thursdays alert. Lashawn noticed that Zone 72 was alerted on the monitor and the employees were scrambling.

She became irate and struck Rebecca with her fist, "Why did you press the alert!"

"I didn't touch any alerts; someone must activated the alert when we left", Rebecca replied.

Lashawn pulled out her gun, "Call Roxie and tell Natasha that someone sounded the alert. Everything that is happening in that apartment can be seen by Oxicure!"

She sent the text. Natasha made her put her hand against the mirror so she could read the message herself. Babe the police on their way over, the alarm has somehow been tripped".

Natasha struck her the head twice with the gun. Georgette saw what happened. She ran to her office and upgraded the alert to authorities.

Lashawn started to panic, "Are you finished? How long is this shit going to take?"

Rebecca nervously replied, "I don't know. We are working on one system. Its protocol that alerts take priority."

Lashawn saw the monitor and zoomed in by the couch. Roxie is on the floor bleeding. Natasha is pacing the floor with her gun clinched. She put her gun in her pocket and peeked out the door to the hallway. Lashawn was in disbelief. She watched her leave the room. Now her heart is really pumping. Her mind is in marathon mode.

"Shit, she left!"

Rebecca is frantic, "Is Roxie, ok? Is she dead?"

Lashawn is trying to find a way out, "Get your shit together, we have to go."

When the elevator opened on the first floor, she saw a group of officers congregated by the exit. Lashawn thought it was a set up and the officers were waiting for her. She put the gun in Rebecca's back, "walk!"

"If you try any stupid shit, you will die today."

The young fem that buzzed them into the building sat at the desk. When they walked past her desk, she noticed that Rebecca didn't return the visitors pass.

"Rebecca, don't forget she have to return that badge I gave you."

When Rebecca turned around, security noticed the gun pointing behind her back. She pulled her weapon and yelled, "Gun!"

The officers at the door pulled their service weapons and separated. They rushed behind anything that they could find cover behind.

Lashawn grabbed Rebecca, "If anyone try anything I will blow this fem head off!"

The young security guard said to herself, "I guess she didn't get the job."

Lashawn slowly made her way to the front glass doors. She grabbed the handle, but the doors were locked. Rebecca realized that as long as she went along with her, she probably would not survive this. With all her strength, she pushed her into the door. Lashawn aimed the gun at Rebecca as she collapsed to the floor in fear. She covered her face. Multiple shots were fired. The room echoed Lashawn's last breath. Her bloody body became art as it slid down the glass.

Rebecca yelled to one of the officers, "Send someone to my house, Roxie is in trouble, please!"

The officer called in their address and was told that officers are already on the scene at that location. Janice hid in an empty apartment across the hall. She saw the officers coming down the hallway toward Roxie and Rebecca's room. She entered the hallway and gave them the description of Natasha. She also told them that she saw her leave and she probably took the same way she came, the stairs. She opened the door for them. Roxie was laying unconscious on the floor. Everyone rushed in. A Med Team was called. Officers were posted at all exit doors. They concluded that she left the building before they arrived. Janice became emotional as she reflected the day's events. She slowly walked down the hall uncomforted. She was headed to the elevator but forgot that she left her cleaning cart in the room she hid in. Before she could turn and walk back towards that room, a door opened. It was Natasha. She grabbed her, covered her mouth with her hand, and pulled her in the empty apartment that she hid in. Natasha pulled a knife from her pocket.

"Why did you have to interfere, this had nothing to do with you?"

It was a rhetorical question. She didn't expect an answer because she immediately began to stab her repeatedly. Natasha was so strong that she was able to hold Janice up with one hand and kill her with the other. Janice sight was blurred as the blood splattered in her eyes. Her breathing was faint because her lungs were punctured from the stabs. Natasha quietly laid her on the floor. She went to the restroom and washed all the blood off her arms and face. She sat on the floor in that room for about an hour. She opened the hallway door and all the officers were gone. Natasha locked the room door back with the key and exited the building through the staircase.

# 6

Vanessa and Courtney have made it to what she called, The Haunted House.

She left a note to Janice saying, 'The only way to find my place in this life is to follow my dreams. I know, that's not exactly what that mean but my dreams keep repeating for reason. Don't worry about me. Vanessa is taking me, so I'm covered. My phone will not work so hopefully I will be back in a couple days. You are my favorite fem. I love you!'

Courtney cautiously walked to her front door. Vanessa convinced her to open it.

"Just open the door and put it on the floor. It's not like Brandy can grab you!"

Vanessa starts laughing. She is still tickled about Brandy locking the doors on her.

"Ha-ha very funny. It wouldn't be so funny if it happened to you!"

Courtney anxiety took over, "Brandy is going to get me in the house and lock the door again."

"If it try anything, I will permanently disarm her ass," Vanessa replied.

That gave her the confidence she needed to open the door.

She placed that letter on the floor," Vanessa, hold this door open while I run and get some clothes."

Courtney walked softly through her home as Vanessa rushed her, "Hurry up, we have to catch the train."

Courtney opened her room door and slid her nightstand in the entrance so the door would not be able to close. She grabbed enough clothes to fit in her backpack and left.

Halfway to the tunnels, they both are having mixed emotions. No one is talking. Courtney called Janice to hear her voice and to tell her she left a note. Her phone actually said that her phone is no longer in service. Courtney figured that it was difficult getting a signal in the building she worked in.

The train was pulling in. Vanessa asked, "Are you ready? Once we start this mission, there is no turning back?"

Courtney confidently said, "I'm ready."

They entered the train and the walk to their seat seemed longer than their walk to the train stop. They sat right next to the window. Out the corner of Courtney's eye she saw Shortie running to the train.

Shortie sat at the front of the train.

Courtney called out to her, "Shortie, come back here."

The train started to leave the terminal. Shortie sat in the seat in front of Courtney. "What's going on Courtney? You and your fem going camping or something with those, big ass back packs?"

She replied, "Yeah, something like that? What have you heard so far about Azavia?"

Shortie put her head down in defeat, "It's been over two days and still no word."

Vanessa looked at Courtney, "Tell her!"

Shortie became defensive, "What you need to tell me?"

Courtney had no idea how to put her words together, "Ok, Shortie meet Vanessa, Vanessa Shortie. This is my friend; she is one of the officers working Azavia's case."

Shortie became anxious, "I don't fuck with police but if you know anything about Azavia, let me know. She been missing since Thursday. It's not like her at all to disappear and not let anyone know."

Vanessa looked at Courtney and turned to Shortie, "I'm so sorry to be the one to inform you, but Azavia is deceased."

Shortie didn't know how to take the news, "I knew they did something to her. I'm going to kill every last one of those pieces of shit! I can't believe they did this to someone like Azavia. She didn't deserve that."

Vanessa replied, "I heard you say they, who is they? If you know anything about what happened, please let me know. Any info could help."

Shortie was stuck in disbelief, "Look, I never did trust police. My entire life, you have been an enemy of my community. Taking lives with the same hands that you pretend to use for help."

Courtney intervened, "Shortie wait a minute. Vanessa isn't like that!"

Shortie was angered, "Courtney, you are not a baby fem. I can't tell you who to hang around but never trust anyone that wear that uniform. I have seen too much in these streets."

"What about justice for Azavia and finding those that did this to her," Courtney replied.

Shortie laughed, "All around Femdom is controlled by one eye. At the sound of one scream, one fall, one rapid heartrate, that one eye is opened and sees and hears everything, even this conversation. I will find out who did this. Fuck the police, I trust the streets to bring her justice."

The last stop towards the Outwards was slowly approaching. Shortie thanked Courtney for the info. She never seen Courtney this close to the edge of the city.

"What are you doing hanging in the slums anyway Courtney?"

She replied, "Nothing, just seeing what's on the other side of my life."

They all got off the train and went their separate ways toward the Outwards. Before entering a no signal zone, Courtney called Lacey.

"Wake your ass up fem. What are you doing?"

Lacey replied, "I'm not sleeping. It's too early in the evening for that shit. I been hanging out with Shae a lot. What are you doing? And don't start lying like you been working."

"I don't need to lie about anything. The last time I asked Brandy how old I was she said, 'You are grown Courtney'. They both started laughing.

Lacey said, "Whatever you are doing, or whoever you are doing it with, just be careful."

### ###

Shortie has been staying at Azavia's shop, along with some of her Web members.

She walked in and started crying. She told everyone," They found her dead."

Everyone started crying. Shortie walked to a back bedroom and opened the closet door. Christy and Jordan followed. Shortie started to pull out a box of weapons. Christy had a glimpse of reality.

She realized that the shit is getting real, "What the fuck you going to do with all that?"

"Pay Fem Madam a visit."

Jordan was at the burial of Elder Anna that morning, "Is that the same older fem that spoke at the ceremony this morning?"

Shortie continued to look through the weapon. "Did she kill Azavia? She sounded so sweet and caring?"

Shortie grabbed two guns, "There is nothing sweet about her. She is a piece of trash that need to be thrown away, for good."

Jordan calls the other fems, "Listen, we need to get our shit together. Since we know who is responsible for Azavia's death, we need to let everyone know, stay out our way!"

Shortie stepped in, "By a show of hands, who here know how to use a gun?"

Only three out of seven raised their hand. Shortie was concerned, "Before the Remnant kicked your asses the other day, how many of you ever been in a real fight?"

Christy raised her hand, "Does fighting my younger sibling count? I use to kick her ass all the time."

"You fems got to be joking. None of you know how to fight or shoot? What made you get in a gang?"

Jordan said, "Shit, we joined the Web so we wouldn't get beat up by other gangs. Its hard out here in the Outwards."

Shortie is thinking of a master plan to avenge the death of Azavia.

Christy starts to give insight about the things that she does have to offer," Shortie, I never had to use a gun or had a fight but I do know how to tap into the cities camera to disarm them."

Shortie was surprised," What, who else know how to do anything?"

Jordan replied, "I know how to neutralize the phone signals."

"Why didn't you fems tell me this before?" Shortie replied.

Jordan started laughing, "We haven't did anything organized."

Shortie hope level started to rise, "Let's ask Bria if they would help us. I'm sure once we tell them what happened they will have no problem helping us."

### 

Lisa and Teja was trying to get Bria to eat something. She was still distant from the burial ceremony of Elder Anna that morning.

Lisa persisted, "Bria, you don't have to eat a lot but you have to eat something!"

"I don't get it", Bria replied as she laid on her bed looking at the ceiling.

Lisa has never seen her sibling like this. She is normally bubbly and always trying to encourage everyone.

"What don't you get? What are you talking about Bria?"

She slowly got off the bed. She looked in the hall to make sure no one could hear her talking.

After closing the door, "I don't get it. All these years and there was no mention of anyone name JoAnne. Now at the burial this fem show up talking shit. None of you find that fishy?"

By this time Tiffany and Tonja knocked on her door. Lisa opened the door. Tiffany asked," What's going on, why are you three locked in the room?"

Teja replied", Where you two been?"

Tonya sarcastically answered," We been eating, oh, I forgot, you don't know what that mean."

"I'm just not hungry Tonya. I have way too much stuff on my mind."

Tonya replied, "We all have stuff on our mind Bria. You always make everything about you!"

Bria was offended at that statement, "Out of everything that was said, when did I fucking say anything about myself? I feel like you have a problem with me anyway."

Bria aggressively got in her face, "You ready to get this shit off your chest fem?"

Tiffany stepped in between the two of them, "Stop, you two are like siblings!"

Tonya pushed Tiffany out the way, "Yeah, I am ready to get this shit off my chest. Why you walk around here feeling special, like you the shit. You ain't shit and we not like siblings. How did you forget where you came from?"

Lisa grabbed Bria's arm to deescalate the issue. She pulled her arm away, "I didn't forget shit. I'm just trying to be better than who my parents were."

Tonya gets emotional, "So, you don't think I'm trying to be better than my parents too? I know what they did to you, and it seems like you hold that shit against me!"

Lisa is younger than Bria so some things she doesn't remember, "What is she talking about?"

Bria pace the floor, "Lisa, Elder Anna rescued us from Tonya parents' house!"

Lisa visits her memory, "I remember when they came and got us, but I don't remember Tonya coming to the compound with us."

"Ask Bria did she see me?"

"Bria put her head down in shame," Yeah, I saw you. I played with you in your living room before your sick ass parent raped me. They raped me Tonya!"

Lisa had no clue that Bria was even raped, "What you mean her parents raped you? I thought our parents were on drugs and Elder Anna rescued us and brought us here?"

"That's true, just minus the details. Our parents sold us to Tonya's parents. They put her in the closet while they took turns raping me."

Tonya is overcome with emotion, "That's the problem Bria, it's like you always held that shit against me. I was a fucking victim too! I watched my parents get killed from a hole in the closet door. Can you imagine being a little fem, walking out the closet and see your parents bloody on the bed? You think that don't mess with my head? Elder Anna left me standing on the porch alone, alone Bria!"

While they talked Kayla burst in the door out of breath Julian said there were Web members coming down the tunnel. Bria told everyone to grab a weapon. Lisa was about to head to Teja's room and Bria stopped her. "I need you to stay here!"

Lisa said with authority, "No, I'm going. I will not sit here like a coward and watch our people die. I will get a gun and stand with you."

They hugged each other, grabbed a weapon, and led the way.

Tonya and Bria put their feelings to the side and headed toward the tunnel. When they got into eyes view of the Web, they saw Shortie in the front.

Bria yelled, "Is that you Shortie?"

"Yeah, it's me, we come in peace."

Bria tell the others to stay where they were. She walked down and met Shortie.

"What's going on Shortie?"

Shortie walked up to her and shook her hand, "I am really sorry to hear about your Elder."

"Thanks, but I need to ask you a question. Lisa said it was Web that did that shit, who was it?"

Shortie immediately denied that attack," We had nothing to do with that. There are several branches of Web, and we don't do shit like that. Do anyone see how they look?"

Bria replied, "My sibling Lisa said she was a tall muscular fem and he had a tattoo on her hand like yours."

"Bria, without a name and a face, I don't think I can help you."

Bria gestured to her team to come. "So, what's going on, what made you come down here today," Bria asked.

"I wanted to tell you that the police found Azavia."

Their eyes lit up; they were anticipating some good news.

"She's dead. They found her body in the Inwards."

Those of the Remnant were frozen in silence.

Tiffany asked, "Who did this to her?"

Anger dribbled from Shorties lips, "It was Fem Madam and those hired hands, Natasha, and Lashawn."

When Bria heard her say Madam, her curiosity was aroused, "Is Fem Madam the same fem that spoke at her burial this morning!"

Those from the Web looked confused. They didn't attend the ceremony. "What is Madam real name?"

Shortie replied, "It's Jona or Joann, some shit like that!"

Teja said, "It's Joann, I remember her saying her name during the ceremony!"

Bria was confused, she was trying to connect the dots but the dots wasn't creating a picture that she could understand. Shortie told them of their plan. We are going to get everyone involved. I don't give a damn if her name is Madam or JoAnn. All I know is, she pulled a gun on me after she had these oversized fems beat me, when I asked about Azavia. All of them will die. Christy will disarm the security system to the Twilight and we in."

With all the talking about violence, Tiffany became even more inspired, "Teja and I are down. We knew something was up with the Madam as soon as she opened her mouth. Bria, Lisa and Tonya, are you coming with us?"

Bria and Lisa looked at each other, "We going!" Bria turned to Tonya, "Can I talk to you for a minute?"

Everyone gathered together and started discussing their plan.

Tonya asked Bria, "What do we need to talk about that we haven't already discussed?"

"Right now, we don't need to talk, I just need you to listen to me," Bria replied.

"All I have done for years is listen to you. I let you say what you had to say. Now it's time that I speak up," Tonya replied.

"I understand that, but can you just listen for one minute. I wanted to apologize for how I treated you. After talking earlier, I realize that I was dead wrong for holding you responsible for what your parents did?"

Tonya fell to the ground in tears. As Bria kneeled down to comfort her, Teja voice echoed down the tunnel, "Are you okay Tonya, what's wrong with her Bria?"

"She ok. Are you okay Tonya?"

"Yes. I carried that guilt around for 12 years. I hated what they did to you but I hated Elder Anna for leaving me even more. I never felt like I fit in at the compound because of that. Everyone had siblings or parents but me."

Bria interrupted her, "Tonya, you have four siblings now, you hear me? Regardless of what brought us together, from this day forward, we will live as siblings and die as siblings."

They stood to their feet and give each other a well needed hug. Tiffany saw them hugging, "Damn we don't have all day, come on?"

### ###

Courtney and Vanessa made it to the Shadows. They have not ran into any danger. They noticed that there were a lot of homeless children throughout the Outwards but that didn't change their mission.

Vanessa is showing her how to use one of the guns she brought with her, "Courtney, you will have to hold the gun tight. The way you are holding it, anyone can knock out your hand."

Courtney started laughing, "I hope you not serious. Who down here for us to shoot, oh the scary monster from my dreams?"

"You need to take this shit serious Courtney. It's dangerous down here. You have been closeted living in the Inwards. Femdom is bigger than your city. There is a whole world that you haven't been exposed to. All I'm asking you to do is have my back just like I have yours."

Courtney smile went away. She started to understand the severity of where she was.

"Okay Vanessa, show me one more time how to use this gun."

After given her a quick summary of weapon safety and use, they continued through the Shadows to the entrance of the tunnels. Everyone from the Outwards knew that this section of the tunnel is a do not enter section. This is the tunnel where myths was created. It went miles below the city. None has entered to tell of the truths that exist below the city.

One hour felt like 5 hours to them in the tunnel. It was dark and the walls was covered with moisture from the drips of water that creeped through the unmaintained seals. There was electricity throughout the subway, but all the light bulbs were out. These tunnels have been abandoned for 40 years.

Courtney wanted to take a break, but Vanessa reassured her that there was no safe place to set up a tent until about two hours in.

Courtney was frustrated, "Can we at least stop so I can use the damn restroom?"

"Yes, but you will have to hurry up. We cannot stop here."

Courtney went to the other side of the track for a little privacy, "Why we can't stop here, all this shit look the same?"

"This area is known as the Place of Whispers."

Courtney whispered to herself, "How do she know all this shit, the Place of Whispers! She either read everything in those boxes hid at her place or it's a lot of stuff she not telling me."

"Are you finish yet?"

"Ok Vanessa, now you are doing too much, I can't even use the restroom in peace."

Vanessa heard several voices echoing throughout the tunnel, "Courtney shut up, somebody coming!"

There were side doors that led to other areas of the underground tunnel. Vanessa had no idea which way the voices were coming from. Courtney quickly pulled her pants up and stepped into the shadows of the doorway. Vanessa pulled her gun from the holster and disappeared in the shadows also. The echoes seemed to get louder with every step. They were both nervous. The voices were so close that Vanessa could make out what they were saying. She clutched her gun and tickled the trigger with her finger. Suddenly, she heard a door open about 10 feet from where she hid. The people that she heard exited the tunnel.

She waited for about five more minutes, "Courtney, are you ok?"

"I'm good, where did they go?"

"I don't know, and I don't care. Let's just find a place so we can rest for the night."

They continued for another hour or so. They both began to feel fatigued. Courtney had enough. She was exhausted, and she made it known.

"I am thinking so hard right now about going back to my house and get in my bed. I rather put up with Brandy controlling ass then to go any further in this dark ass expedition."

Vanessa started checking the doors of the tunnel to see if any was unlocked. She turned the handle of a mechanical room door and it was unlocked.

"Courtney, we can sleep in here tonight."

The room was large and filled with multiple electrical panels. One dim bulb kept the room illuminated. It looked as if no one entered that room in years. Besides the buzzing of the transformers on the floor, it was a good quiet place to sleep. Vanessa secured the door with an old broomstick that she found on the floor. Courtney struggled with setting up the tent.

"How do you put this tent together?"

Vanessa replied, "Damn, I guess I have to do everything on the trip."

She put one of the tents together. They grabbed some food and a blanket and rested for the night.

# 7

Lacey was worried about Courtney. She did call her before she left with Vanessa, but she is used to spending all her free time with Courtney. She made one more attempt to call her but the phone continued to say that there was no service.

Shae noticed that she was distracted, "What's going on with you? You have been acting a little distant all day."

"I'm good, she yawned. I'm just a little tired right now."

Shae was concerned, "If it's too late for you, we can always turn around and find something to do at your house or we can go to mine."

They planned on visiting her parent and then going out to the club. Lacey wanted to respect the plans that Shae made.

"No, let's go check on your parent. We will make sure she good and go to the club like we planned."

"You sure Lacey, we can do something else if you want to?"

"I'm good. Its almost 10 o'clock so we have time."

They drove for another 10 minutes before they arrived to Fem Madam home. It was a lot different from the first visit for Lacey. The red carpet and the bright lights were gone. Now the house has an old eerie vibe to it.

Madam refuses to use Oxicure for their security services. She believe that they are Orders controlled. Her statis keep her on high alert. She has her own security and surveillance for her home and for Twilight.

When Shae drove up, she was greeted by one of Madam's security guards, "Hello Shae."

Shae get out the car and give her keys to the guard, "How are you doing Sam?"

She replied, "I'm good. Is Madam expecting you and your company?"

Shae was pissed at that question, "Damn, I have to set an appointment now to come visit my parent? What's wrong with you. I can come here whenever I feel like it!"

Sam tried to fix the way she said it, "I didn't mean it that way. I was just asked.... I mean, I was asking so I can...never mind. I apologize if what I said offended you Shae. Gone in and I will park your car for you."

Shae and Lacey walked in the front entrance. Another guard met them as soon as they entered the house.

"Shae, can you give Madam a second. She just took a shower and is getting ready for bed".

Shae was getting a little concerned because her parent has been in a slump all day.

"Trina, what's up with my parent? This not like her first of all, to not go to Twilight and second, when have she ever just moped around all day like this?"

Trina looked around to make sure no one could hear their conversation, "She went to visit the Outwards this morning."

Shae was flabbergasted, "The Outwards? Why did she have to go there? She always told me to stay away from that area but she went?"

Trina explained, "Sam, took her to a burial in the Outwards."

Shae is even more confused, "I didn't even know people in the Outwards get buried. I thought they um…. what do you call it when they burn them?"

Lacey responded, "Cremated."

Shae agreed, "Yeah, cremated."

Trina responded, "The Orders allow one group in the Outwards to get buried and that's the Remnant. Fem Madam went to the burial of one of the elders she knew, Elder Anna."

Shae was stuck in her thoughts, "Elder Anna. Anna, that name sounds familiar."

Madam came out the shadows of her hallway, "What name sounds familiar?"

Shae nervously replied, "Nothing Madam, we just in here talking. Do you remember Lacey? She came to the party with me."

Madam said," I remember her. She the one that kept my guest company while we talked. How are doing Lacey?"

Lacey charmingly replied, "I'm doing fine. Good to see you again."

Madam asked one on the guards to turn the lights on in the living area so they could talk. She grabbed Lacey by the hand and walked her to the living area.

"Have a seat Lacey. I didn't have a lot of free time to talk to you the night of the party, so tonight I have more time so, tell me somethings about yourself."

Shae interrupted, "Please Madam don't start drilling her. I know how you are."

"I also know how you are Shae. You only bring them by if you truly like them. That's why I'm asking."

Lacey got comfortable, "Where do you want me to start?" Madam told her to start wherever she was comfortable.

"I was born and raised in the Inwards. Both my parents were from the state of Texas before it was the Combined Territories (C.T.) of Oklahoma.

Madam smiled, "I remember that very well. I have a lot of friends that lived there, continue."

"My parents did fairly good for themselves but not as good as you."

Shae started getting impatient, "That's enough of all that. Madam, she here, she work here, met me here and now we here checking on you!"

Madam replied, "Well, I guess we have to talk some other time, Shae is always in a rush these days."

Madam excused herself for bed. She was up all day and just wanted to lay down and watch her favorite show on PV. She gave both Lacey and Shae, a hug before one of her guards walked her to her room.

Shae was glad that the questions were over, "Good night, Madam. Get you some rest and I will talk to you in the morning. She turned to Lacey; Let's see what she have to eat."

They went to the kitchen. Shae sat Lacey at the island as she raided the refrigerator, "Do you like fruit?"

Lacey replied, "I love fruit but I'm allergic to mangos."

She grabbed some strawberries and washed them in the sink. After grabbing some paper towel, she walked seductively toward Lacey.

"Close your eyes and put your head back."

When she put her head back, Shae rubbed a strawberry across Lacey's lips, teasing her. She then licked her lips before kissing her. She straddled the chair Lacey was sitting on.

"Do you want me to feed you fruit or do you want to taste my fruit?"

Lacey stood up and sat Shae on the island, "I want both."

Lacey choked her with one hand, grabbed a strawberry and made her lick it with the other. She looked around and made sure the coast was clear before she raised Shae's shirt and loosened her bra. While Shae chewed the strawberry, Lacey grabbed a handful of her breast. Now she is in control, teasing her with her tongue, slightly biting her nipples. Shae then lifts her hips as Lacey pushes up her short evening skirt. The security guards that worked in the house watched the monitors as the kitchen heated up. They became the evening's entertainment. Lacey added more spice to the evening snack by grabbing another strawberry, moving Shae's panties to the side and used the bottom of the strawberry to lick the wetness from her fountain. Shae licked that strawberry dry before biting into it. Lacey's fingers mapped the way for her tongue's terminus. She licked her until her wetness became their wetness.

Shae body shivered like she was enjoying an Artic massage. Her heels slid down Lacey's back as she sat back in her original position.

"Shit, damn, fuck Lacey, you melt me, damn."

They kissed and Shae told her to give her a few minutes while she dried off and changed clothes. She walked to her old bedroom and grabbed some clothes out the closet. Lacey decided to raid the refrigerator for some tangible foods while Shae was gone. Shae took a shower and dried off in the restroom. She walked naked into her bedroom to get her clothes off the bed and Natasha was sitting on her bed next to her clothes.

"What are you doing in my room Natasha?"

"I was actually waiting to talk to you when you were alone," Natasha replied.

"Why do I need to be alone for you to talk to me. You already know we don't get along like that."

She grabbed her clothes and started getting dressed. Natasha got up and stood by the dresser.

"That's what I don't understand, we use to get along like siblings."

"Siblings, when? All I can remember is how you always gave me the side eye and acted like you were jealous of me, Natasha!"

"Jealous, how can I be jealous, and we had the same shit. Madam always took care of me. I know I'm a little bit older than you, but I was always treated like Fem Madams child."

"That's the problem right there Natasha. You could never accept the fact that you wasn't family. All you ever been, was a hired hand."

That statement broke her down. She released a dam of tears. It was like she had been holding those emotions back for years.

"I'm so sorry, I didn't mean to hurt you like that."

"Don't worry about it, everybody always said that I was strong, I can take it but you right Shae. What fem don't want to have a family."

She walked in the restroom and washed and dried her face. After taking a couple deep breaths.

"I was little Shae, probably 4 or 5 years old when I was given to Madam."

"What you mean given to her," Shae replied.

"You don't remember when I came because you were a baby. I was rescued by the Remnant and sent to Madam. I thought she was taking me in as her own, but she wasn't. I became more of an indentured servant than family. That's why I hated Elder Anna!"

"Wait, wait, Elder who? I heard that name earlier today," Shae replied.

Natasha became mute at that moment. She remembered the threat Fem Madam made on her life if she told Shae the truth.

"Shae, you have to talk to Madam if you want to know anything about that. I actually thought you knew who Anna was!"

Shae was upset, "What's the big ass secret about some poor, social rejects, that hide for a living?"

Natasha stood in the entrance of the bedroom, "I guess we will discuss that some other time, I have to go."

She paused before exiting the room.

"Shae, I really wish we were closer, and you are right, all I ever wanted was a family. To be honest, you have always been the closest person that I could call family."

She walked towards downstairs, and Shae went to the kitchen frustrated.

"Come on Lacey, let's go!"

Lacey hurried and finished the sandwich and chips that she made for herself, "Why you are rushing, is everything okay?"

"I'm sorry. I didn't mean to rush you. It's just everything about today seems off, Madam going to the Outwards, Natasha mentions the same person that Trina mentioned. Something just ain't right."

Lacey finished cleaning up her mess, "Before we leave, I need to go brush my teeth!"

Shae laughed, "Why do you need to brush your teeth?"

She kissed her passionately then replied, "I know you don't want my breath smelling like strawberries".

Lacey brushed her teeth, and they continued their plans for the night.

### ###

Bria and Shortie have teamed up to bring vengeance upon everyone that is involved in Azavia death. Those from the Remnant has never stepped a foot in the Inwards. It is overwhelming. The bright lights, vehicles, the restaurants, this is totally new to them. The closest they have gotten to the Inwards is Azavia's house/shop.

Shortie normally took the train, but they had to move inconspicuously. The way Remnant dress, they would really stick out like a sore thumb. Outside of the gate, there were several entrances into the Inwards. They took the entrance that would get them the closest to the Twilight. Once they were in it still was a 30-minute walk.

Lisa wasn't use to all this walking, "How far is this place, my feet hurt!"

Bria jokingly said, "No, you said you were ready, I'm going with you, you remember that?"

"Yeah, I did say that and I meant it, before I started walking."

Lisa then asked Shortie, "Is there a shoe store along the way?"

Everyone started laughing. Bria told her to be quiet.

Christy said," You two act like siblings."

"We are", Lisa replied.

"I knew it cause you two act just like me and my sibling. I have always talked her into going with me."

Her sibling's name is Chasity, "You are lying already. You never want to do anything. Every time Shortie come and get us for a job, you complain the entire way."

As you know by now, Shortie love to jump in and out of everyone's conversations, "Yep, she right Christy. You act like you didn't even want to come when we were headed to the tunnels."

Christy felt like they were trying to gang up on her, "That's why I didn't want to come earlier. Everyone is always coming together against me."

Shortie told everyone to shut up as they got closer to the warehouse district. Christy mumbled a couple more words until Shortie gave her that shut up look. They were a few buildings away from Twilight. What they are about to do is becoming real. Shortie already knew that there were no city pole cameras in that area, so she chose that route to sneak through the back entrance. Even though Fem Madam kept the building heavily guarded, their confidence for vengeance outweighed Madam sense of security. The back of the building was surrounded by a 6-foot privacy fence. There was a side entrance but it was only used for transporting the hostess. Shortie plan was to jump the fence, knock the guard out and take the keys to open the gate for the Remnant. She peeked through a hole in the fence and saw how tall and muscular the fem was. She decided not to go in alone.

Christy asked, "What's wrong?", as she peeked through the hole, "Damn, she huge. Where do they grow these fems at? I bet those be the high costing babies at Fertilicom."

They all started laughing.

Shortie silenced them again, "Shut up. All of you need to take this seriously. One of us can easily get killed, so get it together!"

While Shortie decided on who was going to fight the security personnel with her, Tiffany and Teja tied the two strings together that hung from the hem of the habit. They concealed their identities with the cowl and jumped the fence. The guard was armed. She leaned against the metal back door smoking an E-cigarette. She heard a noise and before she could stand up to investigate the noise, Tiffany put her in a choke hold as she drew a puff from the cigarette. It took her no time to slip into unconsciousness. Teja lifted the keys from her before her body touched the ground. She pulled a dagger and was about to stab the unconscious fem.

Tiffany stopped her, "We only kill if we have to Teja!"

Her heart was pumping fast, it took her a second to get herself together. Tiffany took the keys from her and opened the gate and let everyone in the back gate. Tonya went and grabbed the guard's gun and tied her up. Christy followed Shortie in the building and she immediately disarmed the security system.

This place was huge. It was totally different from the main entrance. All the ambience of the front foyer was removed. It actually looked like a two-story prison in the rear of this warehouse. The rooms were secured by thick metal doors and the occupants looked to be confined until released. There was an area that sat in the middle of the rooms. This area was central control. It was used to open and close the doors to the rooms. There were even monitors to keep an eye on Madam's investments. Lisa counted a total of eight guards in the back section of the Twilight. One of the Web members snuck around the front section and only reported four guards.

Bria saw all the rooms and became very emotional.

"We have to free them. I'm not leaving here until they all are set free."

Shortie asked her, "Why do you care? This is their way of cleaning up the trash of the Outwards."

Bria went from tears of heartbreak to tears of anger.

"So that's all Azavia meant to you? You got us helping you because your ass lost money with her?"

Shortie became upset too, "She was way more to me, than that! I didn't want her doing that shit to make money, I loved her. You don't understand because you were too busy hiding from reality. I use to sneak these fems out and send them back to the Outwards. About a week later, 9 out of 10 times, those same fems are back. They have become sex slaves to Fem Madam. She make them feel indebted to her because she feed them, buy them pretty clothes, and give them a secured place to stay".

Tonya questioned," Why? why would they come back to a place like this?"

Jordan jumped in, "They come back here Tonya because there is nothing in the Outwards. They are dirt poor. Most of these fems have been raped or molested already. Now they can at least make some money from their shame to live!"

Bria replied," Oh this shit is living. Azavia is dead and was selling herself to live, that makes no sense to me."

Shortie made a deal with her, "Listen, we will free all that want to go, agreed?"

Bria shook on it, "I agree. So right now, let's take care of the guards."

Shortie told everyone that she will take the first guard. They quietly walked around the building to the entrance of the housing area. A restroom sat adjacent to the entrance door. A guard walked out the restroom. She was too busy adjusting her clothes to see everyone lined up against the wall. Everyone looked at Shortie. Shortie got the guards attention by tapping her on the shoulder. She turned around and Shortie went beast mode on her. She hit her with a fast left and right hook. As she stubbled back, Shortie did a text book spinning round house kick to the side of her head. She was knocked out cold. Tonya and a member from Web name Natalie dragged her body into the restroom. While they disarmed her and tied her up, a voice came from one of the stalls.

"Is that you Monica?"

Tonya gestured to Natalie to be quiet. She stood by the stall that echoed the question.

"Monica, you all going to keep playing with me until I kick one of your asses."

She wiped herself and flushed the toilet. As she pulled her pants up, Tonya leaned against the wall across from the stall. As soon as she heard it unlock, Tonya front kicked the stall door. It was a direct hit to the forehead, she was out. Natalie grabbed her legs and pulled her out the stall and tied her up.

Tonya had an idea. She called Lisa in the restroom, "Do any of them look like the ones that attacked the compound?"

She looked at the two fems and said no. They saw most of the guards in the lunchroom on break. Some watched the PV and the others were on phone calls.

Bria instructed Shortie, "We are going to go into the room. As soon as we get in, hit the lights and secure the door."

Bria looked at her squad. Their actions were synchronized as they placed their cowls over their head. The Web members were in awe. They never seen any groups or gangs so organized.

The Remnant entered the breakroom and none of the guard's paid attention. Shortie hit the lights and stood outside the door so no one could exit. All five of them stood in front of the PV with their identities concealed. Those that occupied the room thought it was a joke at first.

One of the guards said," Get your asses off from in front of the PV. You all play to damn much. I need to report every last one of you to Fem Madam."

Bria took off her cowl and said, "We would love if you called Fem Madam and tell her that we are here!"

They pulled rods from their habit and spread out in the lunchroom. They flowed like synchronized swimmers as they used the rods in an artistic rhythm. The guards yelled for help as they pushed up against the door to escape but it was secured. The Remnant swept through the breakroom until it was silent. Shortie put her ear to the door. It was silence at first then a knock at the door.

Shortie whispered, "Is that you Bria?"

Bria replied, "Open the door."

She opened the door, and all the guards were laid out bleeding.

Jordan was in shock, "Are they dead?"

Tonya looked in the breakroom and turned and looked at Jordan, "Nope, they are alive but that wasn't my decision".

There were only three guards left in the building. One sat at the desk watching the monitors while the other two checked the rooms to make sure the fems were okay. As soon as the two that checked their rooms walked close to the corner of the room, they were grabbed and choked out.

Christy asked Shortie, "Can I get the last guard?"

Shortie was shocked. She gave her a metal rod and showed her how to hit her in the head to knock her out. They tied the two guards up and Christy and Jordan nervously snuck behind the desk. Christy gripped the rod with all her strength and hit the guard in the head. "Ouch," the guard grabbed her head and turned around. Christy stood there shaking with the rod in her hand. Jordan pushed Christy to the side and punched the guard in the face. As a result of the punch, her head hit the monitor and knocked her out. Tonya and Natalie grabbed her and tied her up. They dragged her and placed her with the others.

Bria looked for a button to unlock the door but she didn't see anything. Christy got into the computer and opened all the doors. There were at least 75 to 100 fems from the ages of 12 to 22.

Bria stood in the middle of the cell like room and yelled, "Who wants to go to a place where you don't have to sell your body to survive? A place where you can eat, have clean clothes to wear and have a family?"

Most of them raised their hands as they stood in the doorway. "If you want that life, follow us."

Most of the fems grabbed their things and left with Bria. Shortie showed them how to get home. Twilight only housed 17 fems that night that chose to stay. They closed their own doors and went back to sleep.

# 8

Courtney has fallen asleep in a place that mirrored her dreams. She is closer to understanding their meaning. The tunnels are a grave of memories. Low life's hide and the homeless sleep. Just like Courtneys pillow, the tunnels record her dreams as her heart is left to interpret them.

Vanessa and Courtney have been sleeping for about 5 or 6 hours. Unlike her home, she was able to sleep without being monitored. Suddenly, the door handle moves to the room they are in. They both woke up on high alert. Vanessa grabs her gun and aim it at the door.

Courtney whispers, "Somebody trying to get in here!"

Someone went from softly turning the handle to pulling and frantically shaking the handle, "Who in there? Kimmy, open the door, I know you and Carla in there."

They waited a second and didn't hear the voices of those that they assumed occupied the room. They figured that they were still sleep.

"We going to go down the tunnel and come back. If you two not up by then, we can just meet in the Outwards later."

The three fems that were at the door left.

"That was too close for comfort Vanessa. If this entire excursion going to be like this…"

Vanessa stopped her, "You came too far to stop here. Let me rephrase that, we came to far. We only have about two hours to get to the old mall under the city."

Courtney is still wondering, what is her true interest in helping.

"That's what I'm not understanding, you only known me for a couple days and you underground with guns and shit just for me?"

Vanessa started packing up the tint and the rest of their gear.

"I don't want to sound selfish but I'm not just doing this for you, it's for my mom. All the stories she told me about. Let me ask you a question, do you think you the only one that have dreams? When you first told me about your dreams, I knew we were connected. For years, I had to suppress my thoughts and denied my feelings. When you came to me the other day and said that the nurse had a badge with the name Zia Moore, I knew that destiny crossed our paths. Why you think I secretly stored all those boxes with stuff from the Undiscussed?"

Courtney parked on that question, "I don't know. When I saw all those boxes, I figured what you said about your mom was true. It just seems a little odd that's all."

Vanessa finished loading her backpack, "That's the hardest thing about meeting new people. You have to build trust in order to have trust. I will prove to you that my motives are genuine. All I need from you while we out here is to have my back."

Courtney agreed, "That's always been my motto, trust have to be earned. Don't worry about me having your back, this tunnel is scary as fuck. I will be strapped to your back like that damn backpack you have on!"

They both laughed as they prepared to finish their journey.

### 

It is 7:30am. Lacey is having stomach pains from all the different foods that she stuffed down last night. The drinks she consumed is beating the drums in her head. She has been waking up with Shae consistently for about two weeks. Her stomach started aching as she laid in the bed.

After the rumble increased, she ran to the restroom and closed the door.

Shae woke up when the door slammed, "You okay Lacey?"

"No, I am not okay. I should have checked that expiration date on that lunch meat Madam had in the refrigerator!"

Shae started laughing, "Madam had all that old ass meat in there and you didn't check the dates!"

Lacey food was running through her at that moment, "My stomach is doing flips like the 2060 Fem-lympics. Damn, now its splashing!"

Shae stomach began to hurt because she was laughing so hard, "Now my stomach hurting, when you coming out the restroom so I can get in there?"

"Ha, ha, very funny. I see you have jokes."

Lacey replied from sitting on the toilet, "It feel like my damn foot going to sleep too."

While Lacey sat on the toilet seat of regret, she received an incoming call. She put her hand up to the mirror and saw that it was Rebecca. She pushed ignore.

Shae walked to the bathroom door, "Who was that calling babe?"

Lacey was shocked that she gave her a relationship name.

She whispered to herself, "Babe, oh shit do that mean we are in a relationship?... That wasn't anybody. Rebecca trying to get me to go to work on a Sunday, that is not happening".

Shae was excited to be with Lacey. She almost floated away from the bathroom door.

"I know your stomach not feeling good but I still want to ask, do you want me to cook some breakfast?"

Lacey just flushed the toilet and was preparing to brush her teeth, "Cook, when you start doing that? I think between you and Fem Madam, you two are trying to kill me now."

Shae went and leaned against the other side of the bathroom door, "I can cook a little, I just want to learn how to make the type of food you like!"

Lacey said to herself in the mirror, "She must really like me."

Her phone rang again, "What do Rebecca want?"

She grabbed her stomach and yelled into the air, "Why I'm I being punished this morning?"

Shae laughed at her again, "Just answer the damn phone!"

"What's going on Rebecca and before you answer that question, I'm not coming in?"

Rebecca didn't sound her usual, complaining self.

"Have you heard from Courtney? I have been trying to reach her and haven't been able to. Her phone keep saying there's no connection!"

Lacey didn't know what was going on, but she still attempted to be her spokesperson.

"She don't want to work today either. That's probably why she not answering."

Rebecca's voice trembled, "It's not about work Lacey, it's about her parent. Do me a favor, call her phone and if she answers, please tell her to contact me immediately!"

Lacey disconnected the call and became very concerned. From the way her facial expression changed; Shae knew something was wrong.

"Is that Rebecca again?"

"Yeah that's her but she not trying to get me to go to work. She can't reach Courtney by phone. I think something happened to her parent," Lacey replied!

She called Courtney several times and received the same message, no connection. What does no connection mean? I never heard that before, no connection."

Shae told Lacey that the only time no connection shows is if Courtney has gone outside of Inwards. Lacey grabbed some pants and got dressed while she talked with Shae.

"I have been knowing her for years and one thing she wouldn't do is go to the Outwards. All those that hang out there are hookers and dropheads."

"Did she tell you what happened to her parent?"

"Not yet. I will finish getting dressed and call her back."

Rebecca was sitting in the waiting room of the hospital. The blow to Roxie head from Natasha required several stitches. They were scanning her to see if she had a concussion.

Lacey called, "I haven't been able to reach her either. What happened to Janice?"

Rebecca walked out the waiting room. She didn't want anyone to hear her conversation.

She walked down the hallway, "I can't tell you over the phone. Can you meet me at the Stonewall Hospital?"

Lacey agreed to meet her at the hospital.

"Shae, I know it's still early but can you bring me to the hospital? I think Courtney's parent Janice is there."

Shae grabbed her card to start her car and they left Lacey's house.

### 

Courtney and Vanessa have been walking for over an hour. If Courtney would have known the miles that she would have put on her cute shoes, she would have chosen another pair. Her feet are aching and she is trying to adjust to the cool, damp air of the tunnels. The moisture in the air mixed with the mold is making it more difficult to breathe. Their eyes are dilating as it captures brief light from the puddles of stagnant water.

Courtney felt like she was in the tunnel of death, "I'm so tired!"

She sat on a dry stone to massage her feet.

Vanessa encouraged her, "We are so close. I think we will be there in about an hour. Just bear with me."

She put her shoes back on, "This the worse damn field trip I ever been on."

Courtney complained about every detail of the tunnel. The bugs, stench and the algae has become her focus instead of the dreams that haunted her nights. The route to the underground mall had a deep curve approaching. This was the darkest part of the tunnels. Their hands disappeared right before their eyes because of the thick blackness. They used the rusted tracks as a compass to navigate the curve. Vanessa did have a light but its rays faded in the distance.

It took them approximately 20 minutes to guardedly make it through the curve. Courtney gripped Vanessa's backpack like she was playing follow the leader. She was afraid. As soon as she found peace in the thought of letting go of her grip, Vanessa's light panned across a small figure.

"Oh shit, what was that!"

Vanessa moved the light across the tunnel again, "Courtney I don't see anything and I'm the one that have the light and the gun in my hand!"

Courtney feet have adhered to the track like glue. She didn't take another step.

"I know what I saw. It look like a little fem standing by herself at the end of the tracks."

Vanessa replies, "We can't find out what it is if we don't move towards it. You either have to let me go so I can check..."

Courtney interrupted her, "Nope, that wasn't part of the deal. That's how fems die in the movies that splitting up shit. I should have listened to Brandy and stayed in the damn house."

Vanessa is getting tired of her complaints. They haven't moved an inch. Vanessa gave her the light and she walked on the side of her, "Lets go."

They inched their way toward what Courtney thought was a person. The light shook in the nervous hands of Courtney.

All of a sudden Courtney screamed, "I see someone standing there. I'm not crazy, I told you someone was standing there."

Vanessa grabbed the light and proceeded toward her. As they got closer, the light started to blind the fem. Vanessa dimmed it. It was a fem dressed in an old-fashioned ruffled dress. It was patchy and very dirty. She stood in the middle of the track gripping an old stuffed bear. They walked faster towards her to see if she was ok. The tracks beneath them have become a murky pathway. It was spongy with each step. They focused so much on the little fem that it went unnoticed.

Vanessa asked her, "Are you ok? Where is your parent?"

Before the two of them could get to close, she took the stuffed animal and threw it toward their feet. Vanessa picked it up by its arm.

Courtney said, "I don't like this. This shit don't feel right. Why is she down here by herself?"

Vanessa asked the little fem, "Do you want this back?"

The fem shook her head no and screamed. Her scream was like that of a smoky jungle frog. It was ear piercing and heart wrenching. They covered their ears to no avail. When they looked at the fem as she screamed, they notice that most of her teeth were pointed.

Courtney yelled, "Look at her teeth, we have to get out of here?"

Before they could run away, the ground beneath their feet moved. It was a large net that's normally used to trap very large animals. The screams stopped. They were suspended in the air and covered with mud. The net turned slowly as the tunnel went silent. Footsteps were heard coming from behind the little fem. It was eight fems dressed in the same habits as Remnant. The leader whose name was Shelby picked up the little fem.

"Good job Amy!"

She gave her a hug, "I loved the way you threw the bear in the middle of the net. We didn't even plan that."

Amy laughed, "They were getting too close, so I had to do something."

Shelby put Amy down and walked around the net to see what they captured. Courtney was scared at their appearance. All their teeth were sharp like animal's teeth. They were dirty and barbaric looking. She reached into the net and grabbed Venessa side.

"Yes, she has plenty of protein. Cut the net down and drag them to the complex. Try not to bruise the meat too bad."

Courtney and Vanessa were dragged with their belongings to an undisclosed place in the tunnel.

### ###

Lacey and Shae have arrived to the hospital. They went to the waiting room where Rebecca was waiting. When she saw Lacey enter the waiting room, she was overcome with emotion. She ran and hugged Lacey tight and cried on her shoulder. Shae just moved to the side and let her have her moment. She grabbed some tissue and put it in Lacey's hand. She slowly pulled away from Rebecca and wiped her tears.

"What's going on, what happened Rebecca?"

She started talking so fast that Lacey had to stop her.

"I was at the house and they came in…. I didn't know what to do. They beat Roxie and made me go to work…."

"Wait, look at me. You have to slow down so I can understand you. What room is Janice in?"

She took a few short breaths, "Janice not in a room Lacey, they killed Courtney's parent!"

Lacey was upset. She kicked over a charging table in the waiting room. Security came in to investigate the noise.

"Is everything okay in here?"

Shae answered, "Everything is ok, she just received some really bad news."

They walked out and Lacey grabbed Rebecca by the arm and led her to the hallway where they could talk.

"I'm not understanding this shit at all, who is they and what did Janice have to do with anything? She never bothered anybody."

Rebecca calmed down enough to explain, "They, are the two fems that came to our home and attacked us."

While she explained what happened, Shae received a phone call from Madam. She excused herself from their conversation.

"What happened Madam?"

Madam replied, "Get down here now!"

Shae attempted to explain to her that she was at the hospital but Madam didn't hear any of that.

"Meet me at Twilight, now!

Shae told Lacey that she had to go and meet her parent. Lacey gave her a hug and a kiss before she left.

Lacey asked, "Did you or Roxie know who the two fems were?"

Rebecca replied shamefully," I met one of them before when Roxie and I got a third fem to join us for my birthday from the Twilight."

Lacey interrupted her, "I knew you two were some damn freaks. I thought she was going to be mad when she found out we were together, she wanted me to join in."

"I'm not a freak. That's my first and last time doing something like that. Anyway, it was NaTasha and a fem named Lashawn from the Twilight".

Lacey actually caught on when she mentioned Twilight this time.

"The Twilight?"

"Yes," Rebecca replied.

Lacey is still in shock, "The Twilight with Fem Madam?"

"Yes, why you asking about the Twilight?"

Lacey is about to have a meltdown, "Madam is Shae's parent?"

Rebecca is getting frustrated, "Who is Shae?"

Lacey replied, "The fem that just left".

Rebecca had no idea that Madam had a child. She cautiously finished telling her the story of her day.

### 

Shae haven't heard the news yet of what happened at the Twilight. All she know is, Madam is pissed. Shae pulled up at the front of the warehouse and Madam was standing out front waiting for her to arrive. When Shae parked, Madam walked to her car and opened the door.

Madam got straight to the point, "They robbed me!"

"Shit, what you mean you got robbed, Shae replied?"

"Someone came in here last night and stole my investments. It had to be an organized group of thieves to pull this off."

Shae went into the building and was blown away by what she saw. Natasha was cutting the zip ties on the guards that were tied up in the restroom. The breakroom door was jammed with wedges. Sam finally pried the door open and the rest of the guards came out battered and bruised.

Everyone tried to explain at once what happened.

"They came through the back and attacked us!"

Madam pulled her gun out and shot it once in the ceiling, it was complete silence.

"I will not waste the next bullet. I need to know who is responsible for allowing all my money to simply walk out the back door."

Shae never heard her parent talk like this. She didn't know that Madam even owned a gun. She along with everyone else remained silent.

"Ok, since no one wants to speak up now, I guess I have to give all of you an incentive."

She looked at Shae, lifted the gun, and shot in the direction of the guards. One of them fell to the floor screaming in pain. She was shot in the arm.

Shae was frightened, "Madam, what the fuck you doing!"

"Sometimes, this is the only way to get the answers you need. You can't be soft in this line of work, now watch this."

She walked over to the guard she shot and stepped on her wounded arm. Blood splattered on the hem of Madam's pants leg as she screamed in agony.

"You just got blood on my clothes!"

Madam grabbed the barrel of her gun and struck her in the face twice with the handle. She started leaking blood from her nose uncontrollably.

"Natasha, come and get this grimy wench cleaned up and put her in one of the empty rooms until she heals. After that, put her ass to work."

Madam talked to the remaining guards while pointing at them with her gun.

"Ok, does anyone here have anything to tell me about our visitors last night?"

Natasha stood next to her wiping the blood from her hands.

Madam gave Natasha permission to talk, "If someone doesn't start talking really quick, every last one of you will be responsible for filling all the empty rooms. Madam will cheap sell you to the creepiest clients, SO Talk!"

"Madam, they were dressed like those religious freaks from the tunnels, the Remnant".

Madam was confused, "Remnant? They're not violent. You sure they're from Remnant?"

All of them shook their heads, yes.

Madam anger was kindled, "You telling me that some nonviolent ass. God believing degenerates broke into my place, kicked the shit out of all of you and walked out of here with my money? I need every last one of you to take your sorry asses to the Outwards, find my money and bring every last one of them back, NOW!"

Most of the guards were from the Outwards anyway so they were familiar with how to locate them. They pampered their wounds as they fled the Twilight with their lives.

Shae was furious, "Madam what is wrong with you? You shot a fem like it was nothing to you. How could you do that?"

Madam calmly replied, "So, you think I don't feel bad for what I had to do? I been knowing Sarah since she was about eight years old. I didn't wake up this morning with shooting someone on my mind."

Natasha walked over to Shae, "In this type of business, sometimes you have to do what you have to do."

Shae replied, "First of all, I'm not talking to you. Why don't you grab a weight bench and have a seat in a corner or some shit. Madam, what's all this talk about you being friends with the Remnants, who are you?"

"Shae this isn't the time to discuss this," Madam uttered.

"When is the right time, I shouldn't have to hear shit like this from other people. Oh, I guess I need to find out after I witness an attempted murder and aggravated kidnapping. Let me add one more thing, forced sex slavery."

Madam replied, "Some things I just couldn't let you know."

"Who is Elder Anna and why I never heard of her?"

Madam instructed Natasha to leave, "Shae what type of business do you think I run here? This isn't a massage parlor."

Shae shrugged her shoulders, "I always thought it was a dating service or something."

Madam starts laughing, "A dating service? I don't do any match making. Nasty ass fems order sex from a fucking catalog. I take the poor from the Outwards and inwards and feed them, clothe them, put a roof over their head and make sure they are safe. In return, they sell their bodies as payment to show their appreciation."

Shae is in shock, "I can't believe this shit. All my life I never knew who my parent is and now I find out that you a damn sex trafficker. How can you do this to these fems?"

"These fems Shae, they come from the dirt. They live in the most destitute places. They don't have a piece of cotton to even sleep on. These fems beg me for work because where they from they don't eat. Most of them are thrown away like trash after their parents sell their little bodies for sex. So how I'm I wrong for saving them from that type of environment?"

Shae started to walk off. She didn't want to hear anymore.

Madam pointed her gun at Shae, "Stop, don't you ever turn your fucking back on me, cause I never turned my back on you."

Shae got emotional, "So I'm one of them now? You going to shoot your own child now, something is really fucking wrong with you!"

She put the gun in her pocket, "How you think you lived the good life all these years?"

Shae is fed up, "Madam, if I knew this is what you did for a living, I would have given all this up. The house, cars and clothes don't mean shit to me. I guess you look at me like I'm your property too?"

Madam was hurt by what she said. Shae was a dream come true to Madam.

"I'm not going to take what you said personal. I never looked at you like I see them. You are and always have been the joy of my existence. I gave you all those things because I wanted the best for you. I made a promise to you, and I kept it. Do you know what that promise was?"

She shook her head, no.

"That promise was to keep you off the streets, off drugs and off the beds of total strangers, and I lived up to that."

Shae demanded that Madam answer her question", Who is Elder Anna?"

"Why are you asking about her? Some things you need to keep buried."

Shae yelled, "Who is she?"

Madam with the same volume, "She is your real parent! Anna is your parent, ok!"

Shae didn't know how to receive that info. She slowly walked backwards out of the dormitory into the foyer of the Twilight. The room began to spin as she turned toward the front door. Madam voice sounded distant in her ear.

The strength in her legs faded as she collapsed to the ground.

# 9

Vanessa and Courtney are trapped. While being dragged through the tunnels, they have experienced bruises, scrapes and a few bumps. They realized that they were captured by the flesh-feeders. Their complex was very complex. Vanessa tried her best to count the doors they were dragged through, but she lost track after the ninth door. She was in and out of consciousness as their heads were slammed into the wet concrete after each yank of the strings that sealed the net.

 The smell of this place was horrific. The entire family of flesh-feeders had sharp teeth like piranhas. They adopted tooth filing when all the religions united. They kept the new tradition.  It helped to shred the tough skin. Their nails were like eagles' talons. They were not tall people but they had the strength of an ant. It only took 3 fems to pull them through some rugged terrain. Even the little fem had tribal tattoos on her face and arm. They would make a cut on their left arm after their first kill. This was done to mark rank.

There was a flesh-feeder name Jessica. She hated their tradition and had no delight in eating people. There were times they were able to capture hybrid animals. Since the XY chromosome was eradicated, it was impossible for animals to reproduce naturally. Just like the hybrid fruit and vegetables, animals were cloned and produced the same way. Because all the babies came through Fertilicom, none of the fems realized the damage the hybrid foods were doing to their reproductive systems. The older fems were excited as menstrual cycles became a spec of history and menopause was a thing of the past.

Shelby took Courtney and Vanessa to a large common area filled with doors. This place was nowhere on the map that Vanessa had. Maybe it was part of an underground shopping center. It could have been an old factory in the Outwards. Whatever it was, it had no windows. They made candles, and also used the candles for light. The smell was a mixture of burnt wax and rotten flesh. Courtney peeked through the thick net and observed a room filled with fems. It was hundreds of them gathering, preparing for dinner and they were the entrée. Panic erupted from the depths of Courtneys beings.

"We have to get out of here, they want to fucking eat us! Look at their teeth, they are like animals. We have to get out of here!"

Vanessa replied, "Do you still have your gun in your backpack?"

Courtney was doubtful, "What can that little gun do against all these hungry ass people?"

Shelby walked over to the net, Hello, my name is Shelby. I am one of the hunters for my tribe."

She told one of the generals to go and grab Jessica. It was silence the entire time they waited. After five minutes of silence, Shelby footsteps can be hard walking across the large room. She opened the old rusty door. Two minutes later she was dragging Jessica into the great room against her will. The entire tribe laughed as she tried to resist. Shelby pushed her on the floor next to the net. She pulled out a sharp fillet knife and tossed it by Jessica's feet.

"Are you ready to get your stripes?"

Jessica made it known to the tribe all this time that she was different and didn't want to kill.

"I will not kill another fem for meat. This is not right. We have been rejected by every nation and tribe in Femdom due to this barbaric tradition of eating our own. I would rather die than kill these fems like animals!"

Shelby pulled a smaller knife from her pocket and stepped towards Jessica.

"If that's what you want, I can help with that."

A loud scream came from the back of the crowd.

"Stop, please don't kill her!"

Shelby looked toward the voice; it was Jessica's parent. She instructed the same general to grab Jessica's parent and bring her down by the net.

While everyone's attention was on her parent, Vanessa whispered to her, "Can you help us get out of here?"

Jessica did not respond.

"Jessica, I promise I will not let anything happen to you. Just get us loose and show us how to get out of here."

Jessica stood up and yelled, "Leave her alone, I will do it, I will kill them just let my parent go!"

Shelby and the entire tribe rejoiced. She told everyone to clear the room so they could prepare the bodies for diner. Shelby held back all the cooks, and several of the generals. There were fifteen cooks and seven generals that stayed. Courtney begged them for mercy when she saw the cooks bringing out several large containers. She almost died when they rolled a giant pot out and placed it on a stand. The pot was the size of a garden tub. The generals opened one of the doors and that room was filled with chopped wood. They grabbed a barrel and filled it.

Shelby told the generals," Fill it twice as full. We have to get enough wood to cook two this time."

She walked over to Jessica, picked up the knife off the ground and handed it to Jessica.

"What are you afraid of? You have been watching this tribe do this all your life."

Jessica was sick to her stomach, "So, just because you did something your entire life, that don't make it okay, none of this is ok. You even have your sibling Amy involved with this sick shit. You never asked yourself why your parent stayed with the Remnant tribe and you chose this tribe?"

Shelby punched her in the face, "Don't you ever bring up my parent again. She was weak just like you. I was hoping you would have said no to killing these two. I already had it placed to kill your parent and prepare her right in front of you. It would have been fun making you eat your parent."

She walked off laughing. They filled the oversized pot with water. After placing the wood under it, they ignited it with some type of liquid they had in plastic gallon containers. Vanessa was trying to get her gun free while Courtney freaked out more and more.

"They are going to cook us in that big ass pot, this got to be a joke. This can't be real. All these people are waiting to eat us for dinner."

As soon as Shelby exited the room, Jessica turned to Courtney, "I'm going to get you out of here but you have to agree to take me with you."

Vanessa immediately said, "It's a deal."

Courtney didn't agree, "Wait, take you home with me, I don't think so. What's going to happen when you get hungry?"

Jessica replied, "I never ate a person by choice. Most of the time if I can't find some type of rodent, I go without eating. This life was forced on me. I been trying to escape ever since I came into the knowledge of the truth. So, stop judging me and let's come up with a plan."

### 

Lacey sorrowfully walked the halls of the hospital. She was stuffed with information about what happed to Rebecca, Roxie and those that worked for Fem Madam. The moment she started taking a prospect seriously, she found that Shae is not the person she pretending to be. Lacey was still in disbelief about Janice death.

When she made it to the entrance of the hospital, she called Janice number, it said, 'This number is no longer activated.'

After hearing that, she cried. The train was only a few blocks away so she cleared her mind walking to the station. Lacey had a lot on her mind. She let two trains leave before she realized she supposed to catch one in order to get home. She called Courtney hoping she would answer to no avail. Finally, she decided to call Shae.

Shae was in bed at Madam house. She had no clue how she had gotten there. All she remembered was leaving the Twilight.

The phone rang, "Hey, do you need a ride from the hospital?"

Lacey replied, "I'm about to catch the train but we need to talk."

Shae didn't like her tone, "Talk about what Lacey, you okay?"

"Yeah, I'm good, where are you?"

"I'm at Madam house, can you come here or you want to meet somewhere else?"

"Her house is cool; I will be there in about 45 minutes".

### ###

It's almost lunch time back at the complex. The main cook came out and rinsed Courtney and Vanessa off with a water hose. They were still wrapped up in the net but they had to rinse all the mud and dirt off before they undressed them and prepare them. Vanessa concealed the gun and Courtney palmed her knife. Two of the generals untied the net and began to untangle the two of them. Shelby was in the residential part of the complex. As the net was cleared, Jessica grabbed the knife and grabbed Courtney. Two of the generals grabbed Vanessa. As soon as they got both of them to their feet, Courtney pushed Jessica away. She took the knife and stabbed one of the generals twice in the neck. She fell to the ground. Vanessa put the gun in the other general's abdomen and pulled the trigger. The sound of the shot triggered everyone in the complex including Shelby.

There were push button alarms all around the complex that warned when they were being attacked. Shelby sounded the alarm as she ran towards the large room. When Amy saw her, she ran from her room trying to catch up with Shelby. Vanessa used the other generals that were present as target practice. She dropped three of them as she stepped away from the net.

  She told Jessica, "Get us out of her, now!"

Two of the cooks charged her with a knife, she started shooting. Shelby entered the room and immediately ducked for cover. Vanessa turned and followed Jessica and Courtney through one of the doors. She closed the old metal door and put a piece of wood through the handle so the others could not pull it open. It was like a maze escaping the complex. All the tunnels were dark and wet. Courtney felt as though she was going in circles.

Jessica reassured them both, "A deal is a deal, just follow me."

### 

While they navigated the tunnels, Lacey just made it to Madam's home. She lived in an upscale community. No trains ran through her neighborhood. Lacey had to walk a few blocks. By the time she made it to Madam's driveway she was done.

"Why she have this long ass driveway? My feet already hurting."

She pushed the button at the gate, "How can I help you?"

Lacey was winded, "I'm here to see Shae."

They buzzed her in. The large gates opened. The driveway seemed like a five-mile walk.

"All that money and they can't send a car down here to pick me up. This has been a long ass morning. I haven't ate shit, now my stomach growling like a Pitbull. Damn, I should have let Shae make me some breakfast."

She finally made it to the door. Natasha opened the door and let her in.

"Where Shae at?

NaTasha told her, "Follow me."

This walk to Shae's room was as long as the driveway.

NaTasha knocked on her door, "You have a guest Shae."

Shae opened the door and hugged Lacey. She noticed the difference in the way that she embraced that Lacey was a bit standoffish. She looked at NaTasha standing at the door.

"Why are you just standing there?"

Shae then closed the door in her face.

Lacey anxiety kicked in, "Why you didn't tell me that Madam was a damn gansta? She putting hits out on fems!"

She told her to lower her voice.

"What you mean putting hits on people?"

Lacey lowered her tone, "Rebecca told me that one of your parent's guards is dead, is that true?"

Shae replied, "I haven't heard anything about her guard getting dying!"

Lacey explained, "She said that a guard named Lashawn or Rashawn made her go to Oxicure to erase some footage of them dumping a body in the trash. While they were at Oxicure, some guard name Natasha…"

Shae eyes looked as if she seen a ghost, "Natasha? Natasha is the one that walked you to my room and she work with Lashawn. What happened?"

Lacey became really theatrical. She was jumping up and down and holding her mouth trying not to make any noise.

"That's Natasha? Shit, she killed Courtneys mom!"

Shae was still in shock, "What?"

"Look at me, please tell me you didn't know shit about any of this."

Shae became emotional, "I didn't know shit about any of that. I didn't know until today that Madam was a gansta!"

Lacey continued to explain what Rebecca told her at the hospital.

"While Rebecca and Lashawn was at my job trying to erase the video, and alert went off back at her place. When an alert come on to their home, we have video excess. They saw Natasha beating Roxie with a gun!"

Shae paced the floor around the room, "I can't believe this shit, what video were they trying to erase?"

Lacey was tired and out of breath. She took a moment to get herself together so she could clearly tell the story.

"On Thursday, Courtney received an alert at some judge's house. She said that she saw the judge choking a fem to death. She reported it to Rebecca and she took it from there. Courtney is already the paranoid type but that incident really scared her. Before she signed off on the computer, she saw that same black car."

Lacey started putting the pieces of that night together, "Oh shit! Shit! I saw the two of them on the video. It was Madam talking to the judge and we saw Natasha and Lashawn putting the body in the trunk. Shit, I have to get the fuck out of here. Everybody here is in on this shit!"

"I'm not. I don't have anything to do with this at all. Was the judge you talking about name Camilla?"

"Yes, that's her. Do you know her?"

Shae put on her detective hat, "I was best friends with her daughter, yeah I know her. When Madam had the party, I went to her room to check on her. When I walked in, Camilla gave her an envelope filled with monies. She probably was paying her for what she done to her investment. Shae sat on the bed. That's what I learned today, these fems are her investments."

Shae became unraveled. Lacey just held her until she got herself together.

Lacey tried to comfort her, "I am so sorry that I had to be the bearer of all this bad news."

"It's not what you told me Lacey. Madam told me earlier that my real parent is some woman in the Outwards name Elder Anna."

Lacey stood up, "We have to go!"

Shae replied, "Go where? What we supposed to do, go and hide out like the Remnant?"

"I don't know but we have to get far away from your parent as possible. All this stuff I heard about her today, she is one dangerous fem."

Shae started looking around for her card to start her car. She doesn't remember where any of her things were at. They are scared. Madam is capable of a lot of things, including murder. Shae walked over to her room door and looked in the hallway. She didn't see anyone.

"Come on Lacey, follow me."

They tried to avoid the security staff by going through the downstairs entrance. Its only 4pm but the house sounded like midnight. It was eerie. They made it to the back door. Shae was planning on taking one of Madam vehicles because she could not find the card to hers. She pulled the card out and walked out the back door. Neither one of them saw Natasha standing behind the door. As soon as they stepped out, Natasha hit Lacey in back of the head with a gun and knocked her lights out. Shae started screaming. Madam came from behind her and slapped her to sleep.

## 10

Vanessa and Courtney followed Jessica away from the Flesh-Feeder colony. They were out of breath. After Vanessa fired the last shot, all three of them ran for their lives. It was like a maze getting back to the tunnel that led back toward the Outwards. They conquered the twist and turns. The part of the tunnels that they were captured in was in sight. Courtney was fatigued. As soon as they made it past the point that Amy set them up, Courtney succumbed to the exhaustion. She collapsed to the floor. Vanessa unzipped her backpack and began to hydrate her with fruit and electrolyte packets that she added to the water.

Jessica stood frantically looking back. Vanessa didn't trust her nor her kind at all.

"What is wrong with you? Why the fuck you keep looking back?"

Vanessa stood up and checked the ammo in her gun.

"I asked you a question, why you keep looking back? I think your hungry ass friends are coming to get us. I'm getting the feeling that you brought us to the same place where they can find us again!"

Venessa got closer and closer to Jessica. Jessica was afraid. "I don't know what you talking about. I just helped you escape and you think I want them to capture you all over again?"

Vanessa grabbed her and pushed her against the wall. She pressed the cold barrel of the gun against Jessica's temple.

"Tell me why I shouldn't put a bullet through your brain?"

Jessica was scared. She was born into the colony of cannibals but she chose another way of life. She started to cry.

"Why do you want to kill me. I did my part by getting you and your friend out. I didn't want to be there, I was a hostage just like you, "Jessica replied.

Courtney started to come to herself. She sat up and leaned against the tunnel's wall.

She faintly uttered, "Please Vanessa, let her go. She helped us get out of there. If she was really against us, all she had to do was kill us back there."

"Do you see how that shit sound? Are you listening to yourself, these people were going to have us for dinner! They are sick."

Vanessa grabbed Jessica by the neck and started choking her. Grasping for air, Jessica opened her mouth.

"Look at this shit, all her teeth are sharpened like an animal. We need to kill them all or they will be back to hunt us."

Courtney grabbed the gun out of her backpack. She cocked it and slowly walked behind Vanessa. She placed the gun to the back of her head.

"So, Vanessa, all I have to do is load it, cock it and then pull this trigger?"

Vanessa was angry, "I can't believe this. You threatening to shoot me, with my gun?"

Courtney replied, "You need to stand down and let her go. She did her part. Now we need to honor our end of the bargain. I have your back but I'm not backing you with this bullshit."

She finally loosed the grip from Jessica's neck. She turned around and looked at Courtney in disbelief. She picked up her backpack and shoved the supplies that she was using to help Courtney, back into her backpack. After strapping it onto her back, she started walking toward the entrance of the tunnels. Jessica and Courtney just stood there.

Vanessa turned and said, "What the two of you going to do, just stand there until her people come and capture you again?"

They followed Vanessa silently. Courtney didn't let go of her gun the entire way.

### 

Bria and her team were exhausted. They slept in very late this Sunday. All the fems from the Twilight that followed them back to the compound were up and scared. Remnant was a household name in the Outwards but it was very seldom that any of the residents ever seen one in person. They were almost mythical until last night.

The elders were awakened by the other members knocking at their room door. Julian, one of the fems that are in charge when Bria's team is gone woke the elders up.

"Good morning, we went from forty members to about one hundred and forty members over night!"

Elder Wright who was next in charge, grabbed her habit and walked to the room where the Twilight evacuees slept.

Elder Wright was in shock, "What are all of you doing here and who authorized this?"

No one from the Twilight knew any of the names of the rescuers. One of the younger fems was hungry and she helped herself to some leftover food before Elder Wright walked in. She heard her eating in the background. That sent the elder overboard. She was outraged.

"Put that food down now! You need to go back where you came from!"

Bria and the other fems all heard the elder about this time. They put on some clothes and ran into the gathering hall. Tonya tried to explain to the elder what had taken place.

"Elder Wright it was us that brought them here. That Madam fem that spoke at Elder Anna burial had all these fems locked up in a warehouse. We freed them last night!"

The other elders entered the room and heard the last part, "Did you just say you freed them from Fem Madam?"

Bria replied, "Yes, they were prisoners to sex trafficking. Madam had all them locked in rooms like a jail."

The elders panicked, "You have to get them all together and bring them back. She will come looking for them if we don't!"

Teja was upset, "What the fuck do you mean bring them back. Why is everyone so scared of this woman?"

Elder Wright yelled, "Fem Madam is the reason you eat, drink, and have things to bathe with. She has been giving us food, clothes, and medications we need for years! You had no right going there without our permission!"

Bria replied, "Permission? When did we need the elder's permission to help someone in need? Is that what you taught us, that good deeds are required at our hands?

Elder Wright replied, "Look around you Bria. None of these fems were there against their will. They chose to be there but the way you took them is the problem. She will come for them."

Those that were brought to the house from Twilight has already started exiting the room in the direction of the tunnels. Tiffany ran over to the door and demanded that they all come and have a seat. Once everyone sat down, she closed the door and put a chair in front of it.

Tiffany stood on the chair, "NO ONE LEAVES!" ...We are Remnant. It's our mission to help those that are in need. We are tired of hiding. We are tired of begging for food. No longer will we put our trust in a low life like Fem Madam. For now on, we will take charge of our destiny, fuck Madam and anyone that trade food and clothes for sex!"

Bria stepped in," From this day forward, everyone but the elders will be trained to fight and to defend this compound at all costs.  We all have responsibilities here. Yes, we will continue to serve the elders but no one here will be indebted to Madam any longer. Her reign is OVER! Do you hear me, OVER!"

###

It's been over an hour that Courtney and Vanessa escaped the digestive systems of the flesh-feeders. The volume is still on silent as they walked. Shelby on the other hand volume is all the way up. They chased Vanessa and Courtney until they got turned around through the maze in their backyard. Shelby and a handful of generals returned to their complex. When they opened the door, they heard wailing. Shelby thought they were crying for the cooks and generals that were killed. She walked through the crowd and the screams were even louder. After the crowd parted and let her through, she saw one of the older fems holding Amy's lifeless body. She grabbed her sibling and wept for her.

There was a single gunshot to her heart. Shelby held her body until rigor mortis hindered her movement. The entire camp mourned. The dead was stripped, washed, and prepared. Their bodies were cut and stored in a walk-in freezer. Amy was cleaned and clothe. Her body was prepared for ceremonial cremation. There was a section in their facility where these ceremonies were held. Shelby vowed to kill Vanessa and Courtney and use their bodies as sacramental atonement offering for the soul of Amy. They believed that those that died under the age of twelve are in a state of unrest if they were killed. Once those responsible have been avenged, their souls could rest.

After they had words, Amy was burned. Shelby watched her body deteriorate into ashes. Even after the fire was turned off, it remained in the eyes of Shelby. She met with her generals that evening. They noticed according to their clothing and health that Vanessa and Courtney were from the Inwards. They were going to break into teams early the next morning. They promised not to come home until they were located and killed.

Jessica's mom stayed isolated in her room. After the bodies were prepared for food and Amy was cremated. She waited till the night was silent before she made any noises. Jessica had a best friend named Alex. Alex knocked on the door to check on Jessica's parent. When she saw it was Alex knocking, she opened the door and hurried her in. She looked around the hall and closed and locked the door.

Jessica's mom was excited to see Alex, "I know you heard about what happened to Jessica earlier."

Alex kept her head down. She knew that Jessica didn't want the life that was handed to her.

"Jessica hated it here. All she talked about was getting away from here but she didn't want to leave here without you. Can I ask you a question?"

Jessica's parent said yes.

"Why did you choose to stay with these people? I heard you had a chance to stay with the Remnant but you chose to be with us."

Jessica's parent sat on her bed.

"It wasn't that simple. I was with the Remnant and I loved what they represented. It was peaceful there. The longer we were there, the less fulfilled we became collectively. I longed for flesh. It was a period in time that me and the other flesh-feeders tried to break away from our traditions but we became ill, very ill. There was a leader, in the sect we were in, name Elder Anna. She saw how much we struggled to eat their meat and follow their ways. They taught from a book that was against the consumption of fem flesh. Each day was harder and harder. When other sects started excommunicating our kind all around Femdom, she knew she had to let us go also. The worst part of it all was that Elder Anna, fell in love with my baby Shania. She was beautiful. Long black curly hair and a smile that I saw as a parent that would change the world. I wanted the best for her and didn't want to ruin her life by being a flesh-feeder. When we were made to leave, I asked Elder Anna could I leave my baby with the Remnant, she agreed. For about a year I kept up with her. Then I was told not the contact her again. The last I heard about Shania; she was living in the Inwards with some rich fem. She go by the name Shae now. I wish I could see her again. Alex sat next to her on the bed. Jessica's mother leaned on Alex shoulder as she cried. Moments later, Alex pulled a small knife from her pocket. She stood up and she fell into a state of slow-motion. Alex had an out of the body experience as she stabbed her several times in the neck. She started coughing up blood until she became asphyxiated by it. As her last breath escaped her, Alex turned and slowly walked to the door. She unlatched the door. When she opened it, Shelby stood at the entrance. Alex handed her the bloody knife, put her head down in shame and walked back to her room and closed the door.

# 11

The Twilight staff was instructed by Fem Madam to go and retrieve her investments that were taken during the invasion. Their lives were threatened. Some of them were even injured but the weight of Madam's threats outweighed their pain. One of the guards whose name was Patricia took the lead in this jaunt.

The punishment for failure is enslavement. Patricia led them with that intensity. For some of them, this was their first time entering the Outwards. Their heart was touched at the condition of the people. The children were dirty and most of the adults were dropheads.

If they had rank, Patricia would be sergeant major and a fem named Kim would be first sergeant. Kim was very vocal. She has been working with Madam for several years. She was used as the muscle when clients get out of hand at the Twilight. As she walked through the mud of the Outwards, she was moved with compassion.

She got Patricia's attention, "Do you see this shit?"

Patricia was in the front of the wounded staff. Kim was about four people behind her. Patricia continued to walk.

"See what?"

Kim ran up next to her and grabbed her arm. She was trying to stop Patricia to get her attention.

"Look around, this is poverty at its finest."

Patricia pushed her hand to free her arm.

"Keep your hands off of me. Don't ever put your fucking hands on me again!"

Kim replied, "What's wrong with you? I just asked you a question and you went to 100 that fast. You need to check your attitude!"

They stood there in silence. Patricia was trying her best to fight back tears as she looked around the Outwards. She turned to Kim.

"Where are you from Kim, because you can't be from New Daphne?"

"I'm from up state. I moved to Daphne when I was about 12 years old," Kim replied.

"Well, I'm from right here in Daphne. These same streets that we standing on right now, is the streets I grew up on. I lived in a small house a couple blocks from where we at. So, when you said look around, it made me feel some type of way. I know what it look like and the condition of the people because I was here. That's why I ran away when I was a teenager. If you never lived here, you have no idea how disheartened it is being here."

Kim interrupted her, "That's all I was saying, the condition of this place is horrible. When you left did you not comeback and at least try to help these children? All those at the Twilight are from the Outwards. That shit don't bother you?"

"No, it doesn't bother me at all anymore. I learned how to detach from that. Let me ask you a question. Have you ever tried to help someone and they turn around and go back to the very thing you try to keep them from?"

Kim said, "Yes, plenty of times. That don't mean stop trying!"

Patricia started walking, "You can keep wasting your time trying to be people's savior but I'm done. Kim, out of all the children and parents that I have helped to get out of this place, even at the Twilight, most of them return. It break my heart more when they throw all your help away and choose a life like this. That's why we going to the tunnels and get all those fems and bring them back."

Patricia pulls a loaded gun out of a leather bag that she carried around her waist. She showed it to Kim.

"For every one of the fems that refuse to go back with us, I am putting a bullet in them. I refuse to be a slave to anyone, especially Madam!"

The rest of their journey was silent. Kim couldn't believe that Patricia was ready to kill if needs be. They just passed the Shadows in the tunnel.

Jessica, Vanessa, and Courtney entered the tunnels right as the Twilights' staff passed.

Courtney asked Vanessa, "Who was that?"

Vanessa still wasn't talking to Courtney because she pulled a gun on her.

"So, you didn't hear what I just asked you? You must be still mad from earlier?" Courtney asked.

Vanessa continued to walk, "I'm not mad at all. I just want to get home, get in my bed and act like we didn't almost get eaten by some sick skin loving freaks."

Vanessa stopped and turned to Jessica, "This is the furthest you can go with us. Remnant is in that direction. They mostly accept everyone, so, see you later."

Jessica asked Courtney, "What do I do? I don't know anyone; Where do I suppose to go!"

Courtney hugged her, "We live in the Inwards Jessica. If you get caught without the stamp, you will go to prison. And if they find out you a flesh-feeder, they will probably kill you."

Vanessa impatiently waited, "I already pointed you in the direction that you need to go! Remnant accept just about anything off the street. Just go down there and be free. Come on Courtney, we have to go!"

They left Jessica standing alone on the tracks. Courtney continued to look back until the view of Jessica dissipated. She wanted to do more for her but she couldn't collect her thoughts fast enough to respond.

Jessica made her way through the tunnel toward the Remnant. All kind of thoughts ran through her mind. She only heard of them but had no idea if she would be accepted by them or not. As she got closer she heard multiple voices echoing through the tunnel. The walls of the tunnels were the darkest, so Jessica moved quietly against them as she investigated the commotion.

Twilights crew made it close to the place where the Remnant resided. Their lookouts must warned them when they saw them headed their way. Bria and her team were there and they also brought with them several more fems. They wanted to teach them a new way to protect and defend the compound.

Bria confronted Patricia since she was at the front of the pack.

"What's going on, what brought you to this end of the Outwards?"

Patricia was angry, "First of all, that stunt you pulled at the Twilight last night was bullshit."

Bria and the other fems start laughing. Patricia took that as a direct insult. She reached in her bag and pulled her gun out. By the time she lifted it and pointed in their direction, she had four guns aimed at her. Some of their guns was spoil from the night before. Bria slowly moved Lisa from the side of her to behind her.

Tonya said, "If I was you, I would put that gun away. Nobody want to die today. I know I don't."

Patricia replied, "If we die, let us die but we not leaving here without the investments that you stole from Madam."

Tiffany said, "Look around you! I don't think that your friends agree with you on that."

All the staff started to separate themselves from her. They split up and moved toward the walls of the tunnel leaving her there alone.

Patricia looked around, "All of you are some damn cowards. So, you are just going to leave me by myself knowing what Madam will do to us if we return without her investments!"

Kim stepped from the wall, "You the only one that's trying to bring violence Patricia. I agree with them, I don't want to die tonight. They had a chance last night to kill any one of us and they didn't. Even though they kicked the shit out of us, but they still let us live."

Patricia put her gun up. The tension disappeared like an overcast sky.

Kim consoled her, "What do you want to do from here?"

Patricia shrugged her shoulders saying that she don't know.

Kim said, "We don't have to go back to Twilight. The fems are safe here and we can go somewhere else and work."

Patricia said, "You don't understand how powerful she is! She owns most of New Daphne. The police, lawyers and even some of the judges are in her pocket. When she do catch up with us and we don't have those fems, she will kill us."

While they talked, Jessica felt that the coast was clear enough for her to approach. She walked toward them as they continued to talk.

Lisa tapped Bria on the shoulder and whispered, "Who is that walking down the tunnel? She dressed like one of us."

Patricia and Kim was startled when they heard Jessica approaching. They thought it was one of the Remnant because of the similar attire. Everyone from both sides were silent. They looked at each other as if they were trying to see which group was going to acknowledge her. When Jessica was in eyes view, she tried to break the monotony by speaking. When she spoke, their attention was drawn to her sharpened teeth.

Someone screamed, "It's a flesh-eater!"

Patricia pulled her gun back out and aimed it at Jessica.

Jessica put her hands up in defense, "I'm looking for Remnant!"

Patricia pulled the trigger out of fear. The sound of that shot echoed throughout the tunnel.

Courtney stopped as she exited the tunnels, "Did you hear that Vanessa?"

Vanessa was still acting salty towards Courtney, "No, I didn't hear anything, lets go. It's getting dark."

"It sounded like a gunshot. You are a cop so you should know how a gunshot sound," Courtney replied.

Their conversation faded as the screams of the tunnel took predominance. Jessica was holding her shoulder before falling to the ground. She was shot! She went into shock when she saw the blood dripping from her arm. Bria and Teja ran over and checked her.

Patricia panicked, "I didn't mean to shoot her, I'm so sorry! Is she okay?

Tonya ran to the compound and grabbed some clean rags. When Elder Wright heard the shot, she had no clue what was going on.

As Tonya ran back with the rags, she was stopped by the elder, "What's happening, I heard a shot out there!"

Tonya replied, "I have to go elder. A fem was shot by someone from the Inwards, that came through the Outwards, to find us in the tunnels!"

"What?" Elder Wright replied.

"A flesh-feeder was shot by a fem from the Inwards. I'm bringing her these rags to stop the bleeding!"

Tonya ran out the door. The elder was more confused about Tonya's exit then her entrance.

She ran, opened the door, and yelled, "Did you say a flesh-feeder? Do not bring her here. They are a cursed people and will bring damnation upon the compound."

Tonya ignored her. She ran past all the other fems and gave the rags to Bria. They pulled up the sleeve on her habit. The shot just missed her neck. She was struck under her collar bone. Bria put the rags on the wound and Teja applied pressure to it. Several of the staff carried her to the compound. Most of them have never seen or heard of a flesh-feeder, only the elders. Elder Wright stood at the door as they approached.

"I told Tonya that flesh-feeders are not and will never be welcome here. She has to go."

She wasn't going to allow them access but she wasn't strong enough to stand against the group of young fems. The pain that Jessica was in caused the elder to think with her heart instead of tradition. She was moved with compassion and that is what moved her away from the door. The elder left the door and cleared off the nearest table. Those that were carrying her placed her on the table.

Bria asked Elder Wright, "Do you have anything that we can clean her up with?"

One of the elders reached in the cabinet and grabbed what looked like rubbing alcohol. Bria dampened a rag and rubbed it across the entrance of the bullet. Her teeth became amusement as she screamed in agony. Everyone gathered around her just to look at her shaved teeth. Jessica felt so out of place that she began to cry.

The group of fems that were rescued from the Twilight the night before, saw the staff walk in. Fear showered them. They scrambled around the room like roaches being exposed by the light. Kim tried to calm them down to no avail. Patricia intervened but she still had the gun in her hand that she shot Jessica with. They were even more afraid.

Tiffany stood on a chair in the middle of the room and yelled, "SHUT UP!"

The only sound that was heard after she yelled was Jessica as she hyperventilated. She became distraught, the room began to swim as everything in the room went black.

# 12

The train ride home was totally silent between Vanessa and Courtney. The ride was so divided that they didn't notice that they sat across from each other instead of with each other. Both of them felt that they shouldn't have teamed up for an expedition of that magnitude. Courtney stared out the window the entire ride. It was like she had been away from home for ages. In reality it had only been two days. Regardless of how long it was, her life was changed forever.

On the other hand, Vanessa was still upset about Courtney pulling the gun on her. She was even more disappointed in herself for not finishing the mission. All her life she heard stories about Dr. Moore. This weekend was the closest she ever got to meeting her. All these years of planning only to hit a dead end. She blamed it all on the flesh-feeders.

As vanessa reminiscence about the weekend, Courtney called out to her.

"Vanessa, do you want the backpack now or you going to get it when the train stop?"

Vanessa replied, "Keep it Courtney, I packed that for you."

Courtney whispered, "What about the gun, do you want that back?"

The train was coming to a stop. Vanessa told her to keep the gun. Courtney exited the train but felt the train of dissension following her down the aisle. The doors separated the two of them even the more. She waved to Vanessa. She responded by signing, "I love you," back to her. Courtney didn't immediately know what it meant but she remember her mom doing the exact same signs when she left for work.

Courtney is back to what's familiar to her and she is ready to get back home. All she could think about was removing the unfamiliar clothes she had on. She smelled just like the tunnels. You can imagine how her clothes smelled after the tunnels air dried them.

On her way home, she called her mom. The phone was still saying that she was no longer active. Courtney brushed it off again. She called Lacey and her phone wasn't in service.

She figured that she was hanging with Shae so she would just talk to her in the morning on the way to work.

She is finally home. The door to her home has never looked so inviting. She was so tired that she forgot about how controlling Brandy was. She walked in the house and unintentionally placed the backpack on top of the note she left for Janice.

She greeted Brandy, "Hey Brandy, what you been doing since I was gone?"

Brandy replied, "Hello Courtney, where have you been?"

"See, now you are in grownups business. All you had to do was answer my question but your ass want to be nosey," Courtney replied.

She didn't want to take another step with that soiled clothes on. Without second thought, she stripped right in front of the restroom door. She grabbed the dirty clothes, including the semi wet socks and shoes and threw them in the trash.

"Brandy, what time is it?"

Brandy responded, "The time is 8:43pm."

She thanked Brandy and hopped in the shower. The fresh water gave her so much life. The last time she felt that good in the water, was when she was little and her parent bathed her.

Meanwhile, Vanessa just walked in her apartment. It was void of any noise. This was the first time that she actually felt alone. She dropped her backpack in the middle of the living room floor. Her heart was heavy. She felt like a failure. The weight of that trip was too much for her to carry by herself. All her fears were suppressed as she fought to save her and Courtneys life but when she entered her home they manifested again. She had to be tough for her job. Just like she had to be courageous for her friend but at the end of the day, she was a scared fem that lived in Femdom alone.

She covered her hand with one of the gloves that shut off the signal to her phone. Vanessa was tired of bearing the weight of life alone. She fell to her knees and crawled over to the backpack on the floor. All she could focus on was how empty being alone felt. The shadows in her mind persuaded her to unzip the outside pocket where she concealed the gun. Her eyes became inflamed. The gun shook as she lifted it and placed up under her chin.

Visions of her parent played before her eyes like a projector. Her emotions became intertwined with her reasoning. Every thought she once fought about hurting herself is making sense now. No one love her and her home is void of comfort. All those thoughts gave her finger the strength it needed to pull the trigger; Click, Click!

Vanessa has slowed her breathing and opened her eyes. She looked around in disappointment.

Her reply to reality was, "What the fuck!"

She pulled the clip from the gun. It was empty. She remembered emptying the clip while shooting at the flesh-feeders. Vanessa was in disbelief. This wasn't the first time that she thought about taking her own life, but this was her first attempt. She took the clip and threw it on the floor. In her rage, she stood and threw the gun at the wall. When it hit the wall, it fired a shot. The bullet went through the couch and rested in the wall behind it. She was in shock.

"Shit, shit! I thought it was unloaded."

Vanessa ran and opened the front door. She looked around in hopes that no one in her building heard the shot. After closing the door, she ran and moved the couch to investigate the hole. When she saw that everything was ok outside of some patch work, she started to laugh uncontrollably. That bullet was chambered but it wasn't meant to end Vanessa's life. She took that as a sign to live on.

The hope that she just received, revived her purpose for living. She stripped herself of her death clothes and used the shower to cleanse herself of those thoughts of ending it all. She finished showering and went straight to sleep.

Vanessa wasn't the only person that was comforted by her bed that night. Courtney moved the nightstand that she left in the doorway of her room. She took a running start and jumped in her bed. It didn't take long for her to be overcome by sleep. As she drifted into dreamland, Lacey was awakened by a bucket of water being doused in her face. She was in the basement of Madam house tied up. When her vision cleared, she saw Shae tied to a chair across from her. They didn't realize how long they been there. All Lacey knew was she had a headache the size of Femdom. The last thing she remembered was her and Shae leaving out the back door and waking up to a cold bucket shower. Natasha and Madam stood there as the two of them came into consciousness.

Shae was beyond angry; she was enraged at this point.

"I can't believe you put your fucking hands on me! So, I guess you going to bully me too like you do everyone else."

Shae struggled to get loose.

"Why the fuck do you have us tied up like this! Natasha, untie me from this damn chair! Madam, who do you think you are, some badass that tie her child to a chair?"

Madam silenced her, "Shh, be quiet Shania. First off, I know who I am. And yes, badass is one of my attributes."

"Who the fuck is Shania?" Shae yelled.

Lacey was in shock. She didn't say much because she had no clue what was going on. Plus, every time Shae's volume increased, the drums in her head beat even louder. As the water dripped from Lacey's braids, Madam starts to explain why they were in the basement.

"The only reason I have you tied to a chair is because you wouldn't have given me an opportunity to explain things any other way. Let me start off by saying, Shania is your real name. I always felt you looked like a Shae so that's what I always called you."

Madam walked over to Shae and Natasha grabbed a chair and put it next to her.

Madam calmly sat down, "Did I tell you earlier to leave all this shit alone? Some things are best left unknown. It doesn't matter at all about your reasons why you digging. Remember, anytime you dig, you guaranteed to come up with some dirt. I told you what you needed to know and you have lived a great life without the information that you are now looking for."

Shae replied, "I wasn't looking for no information about you. All the shit you hid just resurrected and came looking for me! All this stuff about sex trafficking, you visiting the Outwards and now murder, who are you?"

"I'm the same fem that took you in and gave you a good life" …..

Shae tried to get loose from chair, "A good life? This is what you mean by a good life? As soon as anyone disagree with you, this is what happens. Just like your workers at Twilight; how you going to make them work for you if they don't get those fems back?"

"I just told them that to put some fire under their feet. None of my clients want them, "Madam laughs.

Shae replied, "This is a big joke to you and this is the good life you talking about?"

Madam paces the floor, "Compared to where you from, yes, you had a damn good life. I lived up to my part. I promised Anna that I would make sure you…."

Shae cut her off, "Right now, I don't give a damn about you or Elder Anna!"

Madam turned towards Shae and back handed slapped her. Shae in return spit in her face.

Lacey felt the wind from that slap, "Damn Madam, you didn't have to hit her like that!"

Natasha said, "Shut up or you are next."

Now Madam was angered. She slowly wiped the spit from her face, reached in her pocket and pulled out a gun. She grabbed Shae by the neck tightly and put the gun to the side of her head.

"Don't you ever bite the head that feed you. I will bury in a nameless tomb if you ever disrespect me again, DO YOU HEAR ME!"

With tears running down her cheeks, she shook her head yes.

Lacey yelled, "Stop, what the fuck is wrong with you, that's your child!"

Madam looked over at Lacey. She released her grip as Shae gasped for air. She put her gun down and stood in front of Lacey. Lacey flinched, thinking that Madam was going to hit her.

"Ok, maybe I can talk to you since this ingrate of a child refuse to fucking listen. I am all those things she called me. Yes I run one of the largest sex trafficking facilities in Femdom. Not in the city or the state but in all Femdom. I have elite officials from around the globe that use my services. Shae you never…, oh I forgot, I was talking to Lacey. Lacey, all those parties, celebrity gatherings, what did she think I did for a living, sell fem scout cookies? I'm Fem Madam, yes I'm a murderer, home wrecker and abuser but one thing you will never take away from me, and that is being a parent. I promised Anna that you will be different. I use to believe that fems couldn't change but when you came into my life, I felt that you would evolve."

Shae is still upset, "Evolve from what, you act like I was some abandoned wild animal or something!"

Madam screamed, "You were an animal. A lost, untamed, wild animal. Your parents were beast that couldn't even control their appetites enough to raise their own child."

"Ok Madam, If Anna was like sibling to you, why would you say she acted like an animal and couldn't raise her own child?" Shae replied.

"Damnit Shae, you just want to keep digging and digging. This is the reason I didn't tell you shit all this time. Anna wasn't your parent, she rescued you just like Natasha and most of the fems there. Her heart was huge, bigger than mine would ever be."

Shae was disappointed, "This is some straight up bullshit. My whole Femdom has been flipped upside down. Now you are comparing me to a wild animal, wow. Who did she rescue me from, abusers, a damn drophead?"

Madam was very reluctant to tell her. The conversations continued to escalate but Madam didn't want to fight with her. She really loved Shae.

"Listen Shae. I know you are mad at me for keeping all this from you but I didn't do it to hurt you. We were trying to protect you?"

"Protect me from who, you?" Shae replied.

"No, not from me. She trusted me with you. Anna was protecting you from the flesh-feeders."

Shae couldn't believe what she just heard, "Flesh-feeders. I thought they were myths....my parents ate people."

Lacey replied, "I always thought flesh feeders were stories they told in school. All that shit they said in school was true?"

Madam replied, "It wasn't all truth. They said that flesh-feeders were extinct, that was a lie. They went underground before the virus and mixed with the Remnant all around Femdom. They tried to rehabilitate them but a lot of the older fems cravings for us outweighed their religious commitment to the Remnant. Anna was the last sect to excommunicate them. She tried to give everyone a chance. Your parents loved you. She didn't want you to grow to be hunted by others who didn't understand them."

Shae had enough, "Natasha untie me. I heard enough for today. I'm going to bed."

Natasha looked at Madam. She shook her head, giving Natasha permission to let her go. She cut the zip ties loose from her hands and legs. Shae put her head down and started crying. It took her about ten minutes to pull herself together enough to get off the chair. She shamefully left the basement. Natasha grabbed Madam's gun and followed her upstairs. Before closing the door, Natasha cut the lights off.

Lacey yelled, "Hey, what about me. Untie me! Shae, tell them to let me go!......Hey, Madam! How you going to leave me down here, LET ME GO!!...Shit, I got to use the restroom!"

# 13

It is 2:30 am. Monday is a day of new beginnings. Jessica has been placed on a pallet in Bria's room. It took them several hours to create sleeping spaces for all those that were rescued from the Twilight. Patricia and the other staff decided to stay the night until they can come up with a plan. They didn't want to go back to the Outwards empty handed but Kim talked her into letting those fems that were rescued, stay with the Remnant.

While everyone slept, Jessica woke up in a deep sweat. She had a fever and shivered from the chills. Lisa assisted Bria by keeping an eye out on her. When she saw her awake, Lisa grabbed a big metal bowl from the restroom cabinet. She filled it with cool water and bought it to the room. She dampened one of the clean cloths in the water and rubbed her down until the fever broke.

Jessica looked around the room, "Where am I?"

Lisa was sitting up next to her, "You are in our room, me, and my sibling Bria. Why all your teeth like that? I heard you eat people."

Jessica moans as she grabs her shoulder. They have already bandaged her wound and used a sling to support her arm.

"So, is it true that you eat people?" Lisa asked.

Jessica replied, "What's your name?"

"Why you need to know my name? Do you get to know everybody name before you eat them? That's what I heard."

Jessica replied, "Where did you hear that mess at? We don't give people names and then eat them. Yes, I am a part of the flesh-feeders. I was born into it, so it was not by choice."

"Sound like excuses to me. They made me do it, I was born into it," Lisa said sarcastically.

By this time Bria woke up, "Lisa, go to sleep and leave her alone. Jessica, she going to keep you up all night with these questions if you keep answering her."

"I just want to know why her teeth sharp like that. I heard they do that to rip the flesh off people while they are alive and screaming!"

"That's not why we sharpen our teeth. Who told you these stories Lisa?" Jessica replied.

"Why did you tell her my name? Now I'm next on the list to be eaten!" Lisa fearfully replied.

Jessica was tired of going back and forward with Lisa. The questions were juvenile. Bria continued to tell Lisa to shut up but she really allowed her imagination to take over.

Jessica showed Lisa her teeth, "Ok, while we were little, we had a tradition we would follow. You remember when your teeth would fall out at about 9 or 10 years old?"

"Yes, I remember that."

Jessica continued, "After we shed our teeth, every year we sharpened one to celebrate our born day. By the time we are grown we have most of them done. It don't have anything to do with eating people Lisa. I have friends and family just like you do. I don't believe in that lifestyle at all. I refused to participate in that and that's how I got here."

Bria replied, "Please go to sleep Lisa, damn, she told you all her history. Jessica, you need your rest, everyone go back to sleep.

### 

Courtney has found herself in a comatose state of sleep. She is laying in a pool of sweat. Her dreams has turned into emotional entrapment. This dream led her to the tunnels again. She repeatedly relived the moment when she stabbed the flesh-feeder. She ran through what seemed like the same door again and again. Courtney was trapped in a horrifying circle. Every time she ran and entered a room, a dead flesh-feeder laid on the floor as Courtney hands dripped with blood. The more she tried to escape this bloody maze, the more bodies she saw. Before she opened the last door, she curled up in a fetal position of defeat and screamed. One of the doors to the room opened. Courtney looked up and multiple bloody flesh-feeders filled the room surrounding her. She jumped up and was standing next to her bed at home. She was waiting to hear Brandy asking her was she okay but she didn't. All she heard was her parent voice asking was she ok. When her eyes completely dilated, she ran toward her parent shadow at the door.

"Janice, I really missed you. I need to tell you what happened this weekend."

She reached out to her for a hug but noticed she had a badge with Dr. Zia Moore name on it. Courtney gently walked backwards toward her bed. The shadowy figure that looked like Janice silhouette vanished. She ran through the door of what she thought was her home but she found herself back in the tunnels. The smell of the mildewed walls is making this dream feel like reality. Her breathing is getting short as she fight off a panic attack. All of a sudden, something out of the shadows grabbed her hand and raced through the tunnels. Courtney struggles to get loose but its grip was overpowering. It dragged her to an old steel door that had no handles. There was a single keyhole that was large enough to peek through. The thunderous voice from whatever pulled her, told her to look through the hole. She did just that. The beast released her hand and she nervously peeked. It was a hospital room filled with babies. It looked like the room was endless. Healthy babies laying alone. No nurses or doctors, just babies. There was a loud knock on the door that caused Courtney to fall to the ground in fear. She made haste to see what it was that knocked. When she peeked back through the hole the babies were gone. It was no longer a hospital. It was a cemetery. In this cemetery she saw several monsters like before but all these monsters were kneeling next to the graves. The sound from the graveyard was like a herd of mourners. She started beating on the door to get the monsters attention. One of them walked toward the door and mumbled, "Find Dr. Moore!"

Courtney woke up. She sat up immediately and asked Brandy for the time.

"The time is 5:22am," Brandy replied.

She took a shower and prepared for work. Brandy started asking random questions that Courtney ignored.

"Your heartrate is high; do you need medical treatment?"

"Did you dream of Dr. Moore again?"

"Are you going to look for the cemetery of babies?"

She ignored every question that was asked. Courtney still questioned how Brandy knew every dream that she had. As she opened the front door to go and catch the train, Brandy asked her one last question.

"Are you going to answer any of my questions Courtney?"

Courtney replied, "Fuck you Brandy! You suppose to answer me not me answer you."

Courtney was excited to be back in the Inwards. She not only missed her bed, her parent, but she also missed Lacey. She showed up a little early so she could talk with Lacey before work. The train came and there was no sign of Lacey. Courtney waited at the station for the next train, still no Lacey. She called her phone, still no answer. This was a lonely ride to work. There was no Azavia, no Shortie and now no Lacey. Courtney walked into the building and she noticed that security had been beefed up. They searching bags, purses, and even pockets for weapons. She rushed to her post and got her assignment for the day.

Rebecca wasn't in and her coworker Wendy was sitting in Lacey's chair.

Courtney asked, "Did Lacey take off today, cause I see that you are in her seat?"

Wendy replied, "I don't know if she called in or not. I been working here all weekend since the shooting. Fem, I am tired. My legs and my butt been sleep for two days."

It took Courtney a moment before she really caught on to what Wendy said.

"Hold up, did you say shooting?"

"Yeah Courtney, where you been? You haven't heard about the fem that was killed in the lobby the other day?"

Courtney shrugged her shoulders, no. She was baffled. Someone getting killed in Oxicure? Who would have ever thought about violence at the doorstep of the largest security company in Femdom. Wendy went on to explain what happened.

"Some big, muscular fem held Rebecca hostage. They said she was looking for something on video that happened Thursday during her shift."

Courtney is trying to absorb all the news. She started to think back on Thursday evening as Wendy talked.

Wendy continued to tell her story, "So after she held her in the office... Wait let me back up a little bit. Rebecca said something about the lady was watching the monitors and saw something. That's when she took her downstairs and started shooting with the police. So that's why it took me 10 minutes to get in the building."

Courtney told Wendy to give her a minute so she could talk to the supervisor. She left her equipment and stepped away from her desk. The supervisor that worked in Rebecca's place that morning was Georgette. She asked her was everything ok.

Courtney replied, "Can I have a minute. I'm just now hearing about what happened and no one has heard from Lacey!"

The supervisor asked one of the employees did they want to work in Courtney's place and they agreed. She immediately went downstairs and called Rebecca. Rebecca was still at the hospital with Roxie. They had her under observation for a few days.

Courtney called, "Hey Rebecca, how you doing?"

Rebecca replied, "I'm doing better. Thanks so much for checking on me. They supposed to let Roxie go home tomorrow if all her test come back ok."

"What happened to Roxie? What's going on? I was gone for two days. As soon as I get to work, I heard all kind of stuff happened. I called Lacey and she haven't answered her phone all weekend. I got to work and police are all over the place and now I hear that Roxie is in the hospital. This shit feel like I'm in a fiction novel!"

Rebecca left Roxie asleep in her room and walked down to the empty waiting area.

"Are you somewhere private where you can talk?"

Courtney responded, "Yes."

She exited Oxicure and walked to a designated vaping area.

Rebecca didn't know how to break the news to her about Janice.

"Listen to me Courtney and listen good. Do you remember the alert from Zone 8 Thursday before your shift ended?"

"Yes, I remember it."

"Well, two fems paid me and Roxie a visit at our home because of that alert. They beat Roxie and took me hostage. One of the fems followed me to work looking for the video from that night."

"They wanted the video because they killed a girl name Azavia from the Outwards and put her in the trash can!" Courtney replied.

"How did you know all this? I had no clue what happened but they still demanded that I get rid of the video. While I was erasing it, an alert went off at my apartment. When the monitor came up, Natasha was about to kill Roxie.

Lashawn was so busy watching the monitor that she didn't see me save the video to an external drive," Rebecca explained.

Courtney was getting overwhelmed. She had no clue that all this happened. She surely wasn't prepared for what was coming next.

"If it wasn't for Janice, Roxie would have died."

Courtney eyes lit up when she mentioned her parent. She haven't seen her all weekend.

"What did Janice do, out here playing shero?"

"She set the alarm when Lashawn took me to Oxicure."

Rebecca became very emotional. She tried to continue the story but she couldn't get the words out. Courtney gave her a minute.

Rebecca continued, "After the police showed up at our apartment, Natasha took off and hid in one of the rooms."

"So did the police catch her?"

Rebecca replied, "No, she got away?"

"How did you let her get away. Why didn't you just give the police her info. Shit you know her name, who she work for and everything?" Courtney argued.

"I wish it was that simple."

Courtney was getting upset, "What the fuck you mean that simple, it is that simple. It's like everyone is afraid of that old ass fem Madam."

"No one is afraid of her. The reason I didn't say anything is because they have something on me and Roxie. If the police find out, we going to prison. That's why I couldn't say anything."

"Where is Lacey, I need to talk to her."

Rebecca's concern started to grow, "The last time I talked to her she was with some fem. They don't even look right together but that's her choice. She doesn't know a good fem and one was right in her face every day."

"Was her name Shae?"

"Yes, the last thing Lacey told me was that she was Madam child!"

The conversation paused. This was too much for Courtney.

"You telling me that Shae is tied in to all this shit! If you told all this to Lacey, she could be in trouble. That's why she not answering the phone! Listen, I haven't been able to reach Janice all weekend. Do they know she helped? Do they know that I am her child?"

Rebecca didn't have the answers she needed about Lacey but she did hold the facts surrounding what happened to Janice. She didn't want to give her that type of info over the phone. So, she told Courtney that her parent was at the hospital. Courtney told her that she was on her way.

# 14

This morning was different back at the compound. Bria, Lisa, Tiffany, Tonya and Teja woke up early and was ready to start training. Kim and some of the others even asked if they could stay and learn. They gathered in the great room and were surprised. All the fems, including two elders were waiting to get started. The five looked at each other with excitement. While they started off with stretches, Teja noticed that Patricia wasn't present. She excused herself while some of the younger fems helped the elders touch their toes.

She silently walked to the back where everyone sleeps. Teja heard some talking coming from Bria and Lisa's room. It was Patricia. She was talking to Jessica about what happened. Teja took a moment and listened outside of the door.

"I'm so sorry I shot you. I really thought that you were Shelby coming for revenge."

Jessica was stunned that Patricia knew Shelby.

She sat up against Bria's bed, "How do you know Shelby?"

"Me and Shelby are siblings," Patricia replied.

Fear shadowed Jessica after hearing that. She didn't know if she was supposed to run out or listen to the rest of the story. Patricia consoled her by grabbing her hand and calmly telling her what led to the present day.

"Jessica, you are old enough to know what happened to us and the Remnant. We were kicked out of the tunnels and had to fend for ourselves. Most of us migrated deeper into the tunnels. My parent didn't want to go. She didn't want to live that type of life anymore. Don't get me wrong, we often fell sick trying to eat so called regular food, but we survived. Shelby was different. She was a lot younger than me and she was destined to be a part of the flesh-feeders. Because we wasn't welcomed here, and she didn't want to follow the others, we found a place in the outwards to stay. Shelby little ass kept running away. I had to go to the shadows and find her every time. The last time she ran, I attempted to bring her home and she pulled a knife on me. I thought she was playing until she stabbed me. That was the final straw for me. I told my parent that I couldn't find her. And that was the last time I seen her."

Jessica asked, "Why your teeth not sharpened and your clothes different?"

"First off, I didn't want my teeth to be sharpened. My parent didn't either. We had to fit into or environment so we had to dress like them and behave like them".

"How did you and your parent get over the sickness and adjust to regular food?"

Patricia stood up. Looked Jessica in the eye and said, "We didn't. Even till this day, my stomach growls for fems. Between me and you, I know a place in the Inwards that you can buy enough meat to quinch the cravings and still live a regular social life."

Teja concealed Patricia's secret in her heart. She went back into the great room. Bria looked at her and she shook her head as if everything was ok. They started working out. This was the beginning of a new Remnant.

### 

Courtney called Vanessa as she left Oxicure. She wanted someone to go with her to the hospital.

This phone call woke Vanessa up, "What's going on Courtney?"

"I hope you not still mad at me cause I need you."

Vanessa sat up in bed. The tone of this conversation triggered her concern. This is the first time she called since they made it home yesterday. For a brief moment, Vanessa felt that their relationship was over. She was glad to hear from her but it also was alarming.

"What's going on, what you mean you need me? Is everything okay?"

"I wish it was okay Vanessa. My supervisor just told me that Janice is in the hospital."

Vanessa immediately jumped from her bed and scrambled to find some clothes.

Vanessa replied, "Which hospital, I'm on my way!"

Courtney gave Vanessa the information that she needed. She then headed to the train station. This walk was different for her. The feeling was airy. She was detached from life. In order for her to carry the weight of all the information that was deposited in her, she had separated herself mentally. She waited at the train station as if she was in a daydream. Instead of Brandy's voice wakening her, it was Shorties voice in the distance.

"Hey Courtney, Courtney, what you doing?"

Courtney stood by herself at the station. Most of the transients had already been taken to their destination. Competing only with the mellow sounds of the morning, Shorties voice still went unheard. Shortie tapped her on the shoulder. Courtney was startled!

"Hey Shortie...how you been?"

"Damn, what's on your mind? I was calling you from all the way back there. I thought you were ignoring me at first until I saw you gazing in the air."

Courtney was apologetic, "I'm so sorry Shortie. This weekend has been filled with drama. It's like Thursday hasn't ended for me. I can't get in contact with Lacey or my parent."

"I thought something happened between you and the cop that you were hanging with. Every time cops are around there is always trouble. Maybe your parent doesn't approve of you hanging with the Orders puppets."

Courtney replied, "No, That's not it. They don't have a problem with my friends. It's just that everything that could go wrong over the weekend, went wrong. Shit, we almost got eaten to top off all the other shit that happened."

Shortie kinda laughed off the being eaten part. She never would have thought in a thousand years that she was talking about some real-life flesh-eaters. When she heard her say the weekend was filled with drama, Shortie wanted to see if she heard about them going into the Twilight and taking all the fems.

"What do you mean drama? Everything was quiet on my end."

Courtney said, "You haven't heard about all the shit that Madam did in Daphne?"

Shortie got a little nervous, "What happened with her, what did you hear?"

"For starters, she sent her two goons to attack my supervisor and her fem. They went to their apartment and literally attacked them. I don't want to keep bringing this up but you remember when I told you that my friend Vanessa found Azavia?"

Shortie just shook her head, yes.

"It was the judge that killed her cause I saw that shit myself but Madam sent them to out to cover what she did. Everything that happen around here has something to do with her. After my supervisor was attacked in their home, she was forced to go to Oxicure to get the video so they could destroy it. My supervisor just told me that Lashawn was killed and the other fem got away after beating Roxie."

Shortie fuse was lit, "She really thinks she running something. We broke up in her shit the other night and she hasn't done shit. She not as tough as everyone thinks. She just have money and get everyone to do her dirty work. They going to pay for what they did to Azavia. I was going to the Twilight later and tag Azavia all over her building. I'm calling her out and that fem Natasha is a breath away from forever for the shit she did to me."

Courtney saw the train coming, "Madam is running things and that's what I'm afraid of. My supervisor said that she told Lacey everything and since she learned what happened, no one has been able to reach her by phone."

"You really think Madam has anything to do with that?"

"I think she has everything to do with it. Lacey been fucking her child for about a month now…"

Shortie hopped on the train and sat next to her. Her mind was racing at one hundred miles per hour. When she heard that Lacey has been going out with Shae, her concern for her safety began to develop into fear.

Shortie asked, "Where are you going right now?"

"I'm going to meet Rebecca at the hospital. She said that my parent was at the hospital. I haven't been able to talk to her either so I'm going to check on her now."

"Do you mind if I tag along?"

Courtney agreed that it was okay for Shortie to go with her. Shortie did what she normally do, talked the entire way. Back at Madam's home, Lacey was waiting to talk to Shae about being locked in a basement all night.

The lights was an alarm clock for Lacey. As soon as the lights were on, she woke up. She sat back in the seat she was tied to. Lacey anticipated Shae walking down the stairs but her expectations wasn't met. It was Natasha. She walked slowly downs the stairs.

"Wake your ass up Lacey. It's time to talk."

Lacey was upset, "It's not time to talk, it's time to use the restroom! My back hurt from this fucking chair and my bladder full from all this bullshit you and Madam got going."

Natasha sat next to her, "Listen Lacey. I actually like you. You the first fem that Shae brought home, that I didn't run away from here. You look like you would fit right in with the family."

Lacey replied, "What family? This dysfunctional ass family, I will pass," as she laughed.

Natasha slapped her and grabbed her by the shirt.

"Who you calling dysfunctional!"

Lacey took that slap. She looked at Natasha, "You don't think the shit you did was dysfunctional. You bring your ass down here and as soon as I or anyone don't agree with you, you, and Madam result to violence. How the fuck you think this is okay?"

Natasha started walking back and forward while Lacey talked. She was getting frustrated. The truth of who they were, was piercing her heart. Natasha calmly stated.

"Things wasn't always like this. Growing up, Madam was one of the most given people in New Daphne. She focused on helping the young fems in the Outwards. You probably don't believe this but she has always provided for the

Remnant by making sure they had money for food and everything."

"I don't know how she use to be but I do what she is like now. She is a heartless old fem that put a gun to her own daughters head last night," Lacey replied.

Natasha laughed, "See you don't know Madam, she wasn't going to shoot her."

"Why you laughing at something like that, 'she wasn't going to shoot her, ha ha.' That shit ain't funny. I'm traumatized from her just pulling the gun. How you think Shae feeling?"

"Shae good. She not a little damsel in distress. She is a lot tougher than you think. Now I can admit, some of the things that she learned about Madam this week was rough. She had no idea about most of what she learned. With all that being said, don't think that she is a fucking angel though. She has dirt under her nails too."

Lacey didn't like the part about Shae hands being dirty.

"What did Shae do? She told me that she didn't know anything about all this shit you and Madam got into."

Natasha replied, "She didn't know. She told you the truth about not knowing what we been up too, but like I said, she not a fucking angel. Did she ever tell you about her best friend?"

"Yeah, she told me that her best friend died three years ago."

Natasha started clapping. Ok, you got you a good one Lacey. Shae told you more than I thought. Damn, she must really like you."

Lacey felt proud that she told her the truth. She started to believe that Shae was really the one.

"Did she tell you what happened the night she died? Probably not, let me tell you. Judge Camilla and Madam has always been close. Shae and her child, Cameron, grew up like siblings. They shared a friend name Allison. The problem was, Allison looked at Cameron as a prospect. I never seen Shae so jealous."

Lacey replied, "Why are you telling me all this? I don't give a damn that she was into somebody else."

Natasha started laughing.

### 

Courtney and Shortie just arrived at the hospital. Rebecca was standing in the main lobby, waiting on Courtney. Rebecca embraced her. Vanessa rushed through the lobby. When she saw Courtney, she ran to her.

Vanessa walked past Shortie, "What's going on, where is Janice?"

"We just got here; I haven't seen her yet. What room she in Rebecca?"

Shortie was looking Vanessa up and down. When she noticed what she was doing, she confronted her.

"Shortie do you have a problem fem? Cause I notice you keep looking me up and down like something on your mind. I didn't say shit to you the other day on the train, but today you can get all the smoke."

Shortie was ready for all the smoke. She stepped to Vanessa and Courtney came and stood in between them.

Courtney was frustrated and mentally tired, "Wow. You two showed up here trying to act like it was to support me. Now I'm seeing that y'all made this shit about you! The same way you walked in here is the same way you can exit. I came here to see Janice, not to hear this bullshit. Rebecca, what floor is she on so I can see her."

Rebecca fumbled her words around. She wanted to find a quiet place to tell her what happened to Janice. Rebecca grabbed Courtneys hand and the other two followed her. She sat her down in the waiting area.

Courtney asked her again, "Where is my parent? You said she was up here, What room is she in?"

"Calm down Courtney. Let me tell you what happened at the apartment first."

"You already told me that she set the alarm and because of that, she saved Roxie. I'm just ready to see her!"

Courtney started to get real emotional. She cried on Vanessa's shoulder as Rebecca stood next to her.

"Ok, Courtney. Janice did help the police to save Roxie. The only problem was, everyone thought that Natasha left the building but she didn't. She hid in a room..."

Shortie didn't like the way Rebecca was avoiding. She peeped that she continued to tell the story about what happened but not talking direct.

"Say, Rebecca or whatever your name is, what happened to her parent? We didn't come all the way here to hear about what happened with Natasha and Roxie had going," Shortie replied.

Courtney stood up after getting herself composed. She walked over and grabbed Rebecca by the shirt and demanded that she let her know the truth.

"Stop beating around the fucking bush like I'm stupid or something. What happened to Janice? I have been calling her phone and it's saying the number isn't active. Spit it out and tell me what's going on," Courtney shouted.

"I didn't know how to tell you..... Janice was killed!"

The entire lobby went silent. Even with the sounds of the elevator door opening, people talking and laughing, Courtney eyes went on mute. Her Femdom started spinning out of control. Shortie was asking if she was okay, but Courtney only seen her lips moving but no words were coming out. She passed out.

## 15

Back in the tunnels, Patricia was preparing to come back to the Inwards. They agreed together that they were not coming back to the Twilight to face the music with Fem Madam. Their plan was to take their chances and finding work elsewhere. Teja didn't discuss what she heard between Patricia and Jessica. She felt that Patricia changed her life so her secret was safe. The only person that still had a problem with Jessica being there was Elder Wright. I guess it was safe to say she didn't have a problem but a concern.

Before they left, Kim a had talk with Bria. She felt a sense of family there with those from the Remnant.

Bria said, "What's going on Kim, why you needed to talk to me privately? I hope no one is trying to start anything."

"It's nothing like that. I wanted to talk to you because I don't have a family in the Inwards. Being around you and the others gave me a feeling of family. What can I do to be a part of your movement?"

"I never looked at what we do as a movement but yeah, I have no problem with you learning and growing with us. The only thing I can ask of you is that you do it from the Inwards."

Kim was confused. She didn't know if Bria was trying to get rid of her or what.

"The reason I said the Inwards is because with all these new fems we will need help. Our go to was Azavia and now she is dead. That was our only source of supplies and food," Bria replied.

Kim was overjoyed with that idea. She wanted to help some kind of way. This was perfect. Bria promised her that they would talk again. Patricia and her coworkers headed back to the Inwards. They chose a route that didn't include the Twilight.

The security was beefed up in the tunnels. They realized with the rescue came responsibilities and those responsibilities brought more enemies. Some of the refugees help create traps and alarms throughout the tunnels to keep them safe.

###

The hospital is keeping Courtney safe by putting her in an observation room. They wanted to keep an eye on her vitals. Rebecca went back upstairs to be with Roxie. Courtney pretended to be sleep while Vanessa and Shortie worked out their differences.

Shortie stepped to Vanessa, "I'm not trying to start any shit with you. All I want to know is, what you going to do with all the info that was given to you surrounding Janice?"

Vanessa responded, "I'm sure that New Daphne police are already conducting an investigation into the matter."

Shortie is upset. It seems like the more questions she ask, they madder she became. She tried her best to whisper a response to her.

"You sound like a fucking cop. Every time you open your mouth you sound like you reading a script. You know as well as I do, that the police is in Madam's pocket. Now I'm going to ask you again, what are you going to do about those that killed her parent?"

Vanessa is angry. She is tired of Shortie pushing her weight around like she is tough.

Vanessa started asking her questions, "Let me ask you a question. What are you and your week ass gang going to do for her. This not the Remnant this time. You are messing with a group of fems that don't give a damn about you or your people. So, what are you going to do?"

"First of all. We already have plans for Madam and her hired hand. We will deal with it without the crooked police department. I told Courtney that I do not trust you. Any person that would wear that badge in honor is a dishonor and a disgrace to all Femdom."

That was a mouthful. Shortie dumped everything that was in her heart, out on Vanessa's feet. She collectively calculated all what she said and summed it up into an equation that equaled offensive. She took it as a personal attack. Now her fuse was lit. She grabbed Shortie and pushed her through the curtain that concealed Courtney's bed.

After a few punches from each of them. Courtney yelled, "Get out!"

The fighting stopped. They both ran to her bedside.

"How you feeling," Vanessa replied.

"You good Courtney," Shortie responded.

Courtney voice went to a whisper, "I really need you two to leave. My parent was killed but somehow you all made it all about you. Please lose my number. I need real friends around me right now and the only one I have could be in trouble too."

Courtney start to cry. Both, Vanessa, and Shortie try to comfort her but she withdrew. After several attempts to hold her hand or show any affection, they decided to give her some space. They walked out the hospital arguing. Blaming each other for getting kicked out. By the time they made it out to the parking lot, they forgot what they were fussing for.

Vanessa asked Shortie, "I see that you don't care about me at all. As soon as I told you I was a cop you expressed how you felt."

"Yeah cause I don't fuck with cops," Shortie replied.

"Ok, I understand that but we focusing on the wrong issue. We both look at Courtney as a friend so we need to decide what we going to do about her parent getting killed."

Shortie continued to be herself, "What you mean we? We ain't doing shit. You do it the way you see fit and I will do it the way I see fit, deal?"

Vanessa saw that talking to shortie was like talking to a brick wall. She settled in her heart already that she wasn't going to be able to work with her. Shortie headed back to the Outwards and Vanessa went to work early so she can look into Janice case.

### ###

Natasha just finished telling Lacey about some of Shae's dirt. She told her that she was going to leave her in the basement for a little longer so that all the info could sink in. Lacey, whose bladder is still full, waited patiently for Shae to come and free her. When she heard the door open and saw that it was Shae, she almost pissed her pants.

"Shae, I'm so glad it's you. Cut me loose so we can get out of here!"

Shae went and sat next to Lacey with a plate of food and a glass of juice. Lacey was confused.

"Cut me loose! Why are you bringing me breakfast like we at the house or some shit? Shae, get me out this chair!"

"Ok, first of all, you need to calm the fuck down. I cooked, brought you some breakfast and the first thing you say is, 'lets get out of here'. Get out of where, this is my parent house."

Lacey was even more confused. She was wondering why she making breakfast like they on a date on a date.

"Shae, I haven't used the restroom since yesterday. Can you at least untie me so I can use the restroom and get washed up?"

Shae responded, "That's no problem babe."

Shae put her breakfast on a table that was across from them. She took a pair of scissors from the draw and cut the zip ties on her hand and feet. Lacey immediately ran to the restroom located in the basement. She moved the chairs to the table. While Lacey got cleaned up, she went upstairs and made herself a plate and set it next to Lacey's at the table. It took Lacey about 10 minutes or so. Shae knocked at the door to tell her that her food is getting cold. Lacey was looking at herself in the mirror. She was trying to figure out how she got herself into so much trouble.

She took a breath, opened the door, and had a seat at the table. Shae leaned over and passionately kissed Lacey. That one kiss almost helped Lacey forget that she was a prisoner of that basement. She pulled back.

Shae didn't like that, "What's wrong with you?"

Lacey is at a total loss, "What's wrong with me, what's wrong with you? You acting like this shit is normal. I'm locked in your basement against my will and the only concern you have is if the eggs are too cold. Why they not letting me go?"

Shae explained, "We can't just let you go Lacey. I really hate this. If I didn't like so much, Madam would have already killed you."

"And you okay with this shit?"

Shae becomes emotional, "You think I'm ok with all the shit that was laid in my lap, no. I had no idea who my parent was until yesterday. I'm falling in love with you. I have never had a connection with anyone like I have with you…"

Lacey got straight to the point, "Who was Cameron and Allison?"

Shae was stunned. When she heard those two names, her heart dropped. She had no clue that Lacey knew anything about them. As she began to retreat back up the stairs, Lacey stopped her.

"You love me but you can't answer that simple question?"

Shae stopped on the stairs, "What do you need to know about them?"

Lacey replied, "Who were they?"

"You keep asking in past tense so you already have info on them. You just want to see if I will tell the truth. So let me answer the question. Cameron was my best friend. As you know, she is the child of Judge Camilla. Allison was a friend. I was really into Allison but she liked Cameron. When I saw that I couldn't have Allison, I set up the both of them. I invited Allison first to a hotel and I fucked the shit out of her. See, I knew she was curious about eye drops so I gave her some. Besides you, the sex was fire, damn. By the time Cameron showed up, we were done. I was through with her. I told her to go ahead and get naked so she could see what it was like to sit on Allison face but she didn't want that. She tried to leave. As soon as she opened the door, I snatched her ass back into the room. Her clumsy ass hit the back of her head on the table. She was knocked out cold. I didn't want her to tell anyone about what happened so I overdosed Allison with drops. Me and Natasha and Lashawn put her in the trunk and headed to the Outwards. She woke up in the trunk and started kicking and screaming. Natasha stopped the car and started punching her in the face until she was silent. Lashawn grabbed the drops and put it in both eyes and put her next to an empty house. We figured that she wouldn't tell anyone because of embarrassment. The only problem was, Lashawn gave her a deadly damn dose. They found her dead the next day."

Lacey shamefully said, "So Natasha was telling the truth about you."

"Natasha, she always telling. Well since you know this about me, I guess you don't want to be with me now."

Lacey chose her words carefully. She couldn't tell her that she didn't want to be with her because she could end up like Allison. She decided to play it safe.

"Shae, before we found out all this shit happened, you were all I thought off. Even after finding out what Natasha did to my friend parent, I still came to see you. I was enjoying our times together. I think you have a fucked-up family and hope the police arrest Natasha for what she did but I still want you."

Shae eyes swelled with tears. She walked over to Lacey and straddled her.

"If I let you go, will you tell the police what I did?"

"If you let me go, I'm going straight to Courtney house so I can be there for her. I don't have anything to do with that. On the other hand, everyone knows about Natasha. Pretty soon, they will find her. Shae, let me go. I don't want to be stuck down here in the basement another night."

Shae stood up, "I will make a deal with you. If you eat all this food I made for you, we will revisit you leaving."

### 

Shortie gathered her crew and they were headed down the tunnels to talk to Bria. The Web was already in agreement with Shortie that something had to be done with Fem Madam. They were ready to go to war, with the help of Remnant. When the Remnant lookouts saw the Web, they sounded the alarm. The faithful five grabbed their weapons and went to defend the compound. They rushed down the tunnels and Shortie yelled to them.

"It's Shortie and we need your help."

Bria and her team gathered around as Shortie explained.

"A friend of mine that witnessed what happened to Azavia is in trouble. Madam and Natasha killed her parent. Now Courtney can't find her fem that's banging Madam's child."

Teja was upset, "I'm tired of hearing about her. She came to Elder Anna burial and gave that little speech like she was honoring her. If we knew she was that evil, she never would have spoken. This time, we need to get everyone involved."

They sat in the tunnels and came up with a plan to attack Madam and bring down her organization.

### 

The Remnant and the Web wasn't the only ones conspiring. Shelby and a handful of her generals were still trying to locate Courtney and Vanessa in the Inwards. The flesh-feeders made all kind of wax works to make money to survive. The face of the company was a flesh-feeder name Susan Duncan. She owned a company called Wax Delights. Susan has been in the inwards for years. She was groomed to be in the position she was in. Her parent didn't allow her to partake in the traditions of tooth sharpening and other things. Because she been in the inwards so long, she became a functional flesh-feeder. That mean that she didn't get sick if she hasn't had fem meat.

Susan heard about what happened and have done some research to find out the names and residents of Courtney and Vanessa. Shelby paid Susan a visit.

"Why are you roaming around this time of day in the Inwards, do you have a death wish or something?"

Shelby was at a loss for words because of the grief she bore.

"I know my life is at risk every time I come to the Inwards. The only problem is, I don't give a fuck Susan. They killed Amy!"

Susan replied, "I know Shelby but New Daphne is a big city. I did find out their names, that's a start. Now I will give you their names but you have to agree to go home until I can get more info on them."

Shelby thought about it and agreed.

"Their names are Courtney and Vanessa. I don't know where they live or work but give me a few more days and I will know everything about them, even their address.

Shelby felt relieved. They snuck back to the tunnels.

# 16

Courtney has just arrived home, alone. Everything that she did on her weekend hiatus replayed in the front of her mind like a movie on the eternal journey home. She also remembered placing the letter to Janice on the floor. As soon as she walked in, she lifted the backpack from the floor. She picked up the letter that she left for Janice and opened it. She read it to herself. Her heart was broken. This was the longest day of her life. Courtney has had several calls from Vanessa but she just ignored it.

Brandy asked her, "Do you need medical attention? I noticed that your heart rhythm has changed drastically?"

Courtney wasn't in the mood to argue.

She mumbled, "No, I don't need medical attention. I need my parent. Can you bring her back?"

"I'm so sorry Courtney, I cannot bring Janice back. Her phone says that she is no longer active. Is there anything else I can do?"

Courtney told Brandy to sign off. She laid across the floor sobbing. She was in disbelief. The only way to get out of this nightmare was to wake up. She got up and walked to the kitchen. She reached in the drawer where the utensils were kept. Courtney reached for a knife and was spooked. Fear caused her to jump back. Her hands were shaking and she started to convince herself that she was dreaming.

"This is just a dream; this is just a dream."

It was as though time had stopped. She had no idea that she stood in that same spot for 45 minutes. After gazing at the draw, her decision was made. Courtney grabbed the sharpest knife in contemplation of cutting her wrist. Her phone rang. She put her hand against the glass cabinet door and saw that it was Vanessa, she ignored it. Courtney was standing there, encouraging herself to take her own life.

"You got this. Just take the knife and slice it below the wrist. You will have a chance to be with Janice, do it!"

The voices in her mind was compelling her to end it all. She was hesitant because her heart was telling her not to do it. By the time she looked down at her wrist, it was already etched up. She subconsciously wrote out her pain with the tip of the knife all over her forearm. Her Femdom was spinning. Echoes of her parents' voice soothed the pounding of her heart. As soon as she calmed down enough to think rationally, her rage was ignited as a brief aroma of Janice's favorite perfume lingered in the kitchen. The scent became imprisoned in her nostrils. Her anger was loosed again. She clinched the metal handle of the knife. Brandy was activated.

"Courtney please put the knife down. I cannot protect you if you are the one intending to hurt yourself. This is not what your parent would want you to do!"

Courtney emotionally responded, "How the fuck you know what she wanted. You think you know every fucking thing."

"I don't know everything but she left me a message to give to you."

She dropped the knife. Courtney was confused on what she just heard.

"Did you just say that Janice left you a message to give to me?"

"Yes she did."

She began to pace the floor.

"Brandy, I hope you not making this shit up. When did she leave this message!"

Brandy replied, "Janice left a message for you Saturday when you left for the Outwards."

Everything went silent.

Courtney impatiently waited for a response.

"What did she say?"

Courtney had a tsunami of emotions. Janice being murdered was overwhelming enough and now Brandy telling her that she have a message was disheartening.

Brandy played the message with her parent's recorded voice.

"Dear Courtney, if you hearing this message it could only mean something unforeseen has happened to me. I don't even know why I'm leaving this message with Brandy but I really feel compelled today to do so (Janice got emotional). I love you so much Courtney. All those dreams was conformation that the gods have a plan for you. Those are not dreams to scare you but dreams to guide you. I really feel like this is the furthest that I will be able to go with you on this journey called life. One thing I need you to do is tell Zia I said hi and when you find JD (she starts crying) just tell them that I miss them so much. Don't be afraid to step into your destiny. You are stronger than you think and I love you with all my heart."

Courtney sat quietly on the kitchen floor for about 10 minutes.

"Brandy, I need you to store that message in your memory bank."

She stood up and grabbed the knife off the floor. She burst out in laughter. The thought of cutting her wrist was now humorous. As soon as she put the knife in the sink, she heard someone beating on the door.

"Courtney, open the door! Please, open the door!"

Courtney rushed to the door and opened it. She was hoping it was Lacey. To her surprise, it was Vanessa. She was out of breath from running from the train to her house. As soon as the door opened, she rushed in and embraced her.

"What are you doing here Vanessa?"

She was still trying to catch her breath, "I know how it feel to be alone when I loss my parent. Even though you kicked me and Shortie out the hospital, I still consider you as a friend. Courtney, I really want to be here for you. I'm sorry for trying to make things about me all the time. In this short ass period of time that we have known each other, we have been through some real shit. All I'm saying is, I want to keep going through weird shit with you."

"It's okay Vanessa. We will be forever cool."

She closed the door and attempted to call Lacey. Vanessa was as concerned as she was.

###

Lacey was more concerned than Courtney and Vanessa put together. The basement has been her home for almost a full day. She was at least freed to use the restroom. For the past hour and a half, she has been trying to find a way out and searching for a weapon. Lacey is blaming herself. Bad decisions about choosing fems has always been her burden. That's the reason why she never commits to any relationships. Always in fear that it will be the wrong person.

Lacey heard the doorknob unlocking. She sat at the table with her head down like she was sleep. Madam, Natasha, and Shae walked in together. Natasha woke her up.

"Lacey, stop faking and wake your ass up."

She picked her head up, like she just woke up.

Natasha, started laughing, "You know we can watch everything your stupid ass doing down here from the cameras."

Lacey spoke out, "Madam, can you please let me go? I didn't see shit and I'm not telling shit. I just want to go home!"

Madam insisted that Lacey have a seat next to her. Madam promised her that she will let her leave as soon as she is finished talking.

"Okay, let me tell you something about me. First of all, my word is my bond. If I say I will let you go, I will let you go."

Shae didn't like what she heard. What she heard was Lacey was leaving her for good.

"How are you going to just let her go? I don't want her to leave me!"

Madam got upset, "Shae, you can't make anyone love you. I don't know where you got that shit from. If Lacey want to be with you, even after learning all this shit about your family, it's her choice. I didn't lock her down her for you. I wanted to see if she was going to go to the police when she leave but she already know I own them too. Now back to what I was saying, I will let you go. I told you before that I like you. And because I like you, I need you to stay out my way. I'm about to move through this city and clean all the shit that has gathered over the last couple days. My help hasn't helped at all. They just made it harder for me due to all there fuck ups. Lacey, I will have Shae to bring you some lunch and after that, you can go. I will have Shae to drop you off."

The three of them left the basement. Shae was notably upset. Madam confronted her about her attitude.

"What is your problem Shae?"

Shae replied, "She not coming back. If you let her go, she will leave me forever and it's like no one give a damn."

Madam is appalled, "If we let her go? Do you hear yourself? You sound dumb ass fuck! Look at me Shae. You will never know what you have until you let it go. Let her go."

Shae starts crying. Madam turns her attention to Natasha.

"I have no idea what you two were doing but your actions turned the heat up. I heard you killed a woman that had nothing to do with any of this."

Natasha tried to defend her actions but she was immediately shut down.

"Shut up Natasha. I don't want to hear any more excuses. You killed Lacey best friend parent. What were you thinking that all this was going to just, go away. The only reason I'm letting Lacey go is so she can lead us to her friend."

Shae was in shock when she heard that, "So once she lead you to her friend, then what?"

"Shae, let me deal with the details. Natasha, run and get her some lunch so we can get ready to let her go."

### 

Courtney and Vanessa are still at her home trying to figure out how to get in contact with Lacey. They thought that she was dead but if she was her phone would say, no longer active. They sat down in her living room and brainstormed. Since her identITy was connected to her phone, she asked Brandy a few questions.

"Brandy, while I was gone, did I get any phone calls or messages from Lacey?"

Brandy replied, "She had 17 unsuccessful attempts and one projected message."

"Pull up the projected message."

When brandy pulled the messages up, it was pictures of Madam house. When she went to Madam house for the first time, she sent those pics to show off where she was at. Vanessa zoomed in on one of the photos and was able to get the address.

"We got the address. I can go to work and get some information and make sure this is accurate."

Vanessa hugged her and told her to get some rest. She also reassured her that they will find Lacey. Vanessa ran and took the first train headed out. She was going to go to the police station and get the info she needed. Her mind was preoccupied. She didn't even notice Shortie running to jump on the train. She sat down right next to her.

Vanessa was startled, "Where are you headed to Shortie?"

"I'm headed to the hospital to see Courtney, why what's going on?"

"She isn't at the hospital, she is home. I just left her. I'm headed to the office (she looks around). I think we have the address to Madam house."

Shortie was excited, "That's what I was going to ask her about. Let me have the address. I have some people that's going with me to handle that little situation."

Vanessa didn't get along with Shortie but she didn't want anything to happen to her. She gave her the address to Madam estate.

Vanessa said, "I know that you and your posse' can handle yourself, but Madam is out of your league."

"What are you trying to say," Shortie replied.

"All I'm saying is, let me help. I want to take them down as much as you do but the neighborhood she live in, you will be outgunned and outnumbered. Let me help."

Shortie agreed to let her help. She told her about her plans with Bria and her team. With the address, they could attack them tonight. Vanessa was willing to help but she would have to conceal her identity. After they went their separate ways, Vanessa called Courtney.

"I just want to let you know that Shortie and I are working together to get everyone involved with Janice death. Shortie and her people will pay Madam a visit as soon as the street lights flicker. Don't worry, if Lacey is there, they will bring her home.

### 

It is about 4:30pm. Shortie told Bria and all that wanted to help take Madam down, to meet her at Azavia's shop. She made it back to the Outwards right on time. Bria took several other fems with her. With the address in hand, Shortie planned to strike at sundown. Everyone was armed that knew how to handle a gun. Christie was responsible for the alarms again. They were better prepared this time and they walked with a new confidence.

Shortie mapped out the home of Madam. She estimated five armed guards on duty. They strategically planned a smooth entrance and exit. They wanted to make sure that Madam wouldn't make it out alive. The Remnants entire mission was to avenge the death of Azavia. They still haven't identified the fem from the Web that killed Elder Anna. Even though it was Natasha, Lisa hasn't had a chance to see her in real time. They were going to head inward at sunset.

### 

Shae went downstairs in the basement. She was in search of the vibe that her and Lacey shared. Lacey sat at the table. She just finished eating the food that Natasha brought to her. With everything she just learned, she doesn't know what to think. Shae didn't know about all the illegal stuff that Madam was in to but her thoughts were mixed.

Shae pulled a seat up next to her. She just stared at Lacey and didn't say a word. Lacey felt uncomfortable.

"Shae, why are you just staring at me?"

"Because I don't want us to end. I finally found someone that I really care about. I am in love with you Lacey. I'm just as surprised about all the shit Madam is into but if it was your family, what would you do?"

Lacey responded, "If I had a family that was twisted like yours, I don't know what I would do. One thing I do know Shae is I'm really into you. Why don't you just leave with me when I go?"

Shae replied, "I want to. I want to be with you for the rest of my life but right now, Madam will not let me leave with you. We have to wait till everything dies down. Anyway, you talked about Courtney all weekend, please go, and check on her. I heard about what Natasha did and I don't fucking agree with nothing she done. Courtney's parent had nothing to do with their shit."

Shae walked behind Lacey and hugged her from the back. Lacey turned her chair around. She was now face to face with her. They cautiously kissed. After a few pecks, their embrace became more intimate. They couldn't keep their hands off each other. Lacey pushed the empty containers that was on the table to the floor. She laid Shae across the table like a Thanksgiving spread. She peeled her shirt off of her and placed it over the camera in the basement. Shae removed her shorts. Lacey climbed on top of her and used her entire body as a kissing post. Shae stretched across the table like a crucifix. Every piece of her soul was accessed completely at the will of Lacey. She spent the next 10 minutes taking her time to find every pleasure point imaginable from her breast down to her thighs. If the cameras were not blocked, it would look like an exorcism. Shae's body levitated each time Lacey's tongue caused her clit to spasm. Lacey stood next to the table and spun her around like a top. Her face landed in between her thighs again. Shae almost pulled out some of Lacey's braids as she reached her climax. The heavy breathing has slowed. Lacey grabs Shae shirt off the camera. She turned around and Shae is in tears.

Shae uttered, "Don't leave me Lacey. I don't want anyone else but you. I understand you have a lot to think about but please consider that I'm just finding out all this stuff too.

Lacey stops her, "Shae, listen to me. All I want to do is, go home, get out these clothes, and take me a shower. That's it. We will talk like we normally do. Just let me get cleaned up and sleep in my bed."

She finished getting dressed. Lacey gave her another passionate kiss as Natasha opened the basement door.

"Shae, Madam said that we were leaving in a few minutes so get ready."

### 

Shortie and all those that came with her are ready. They came through another part of the Outwards to reach Madam's place. The Elite mostly lived in the central parts of the cities. Madam, Natasha, Shae, and Lacey is pulling out the driveway. It will take them about 30 minutes to drop her off and to get back home.

In order for the Remnant to not be seen, they had to walk through the darkest parts of their community and that was the alleyway. Everyone is nervous. Shortie and her crew witnessed something they never seen before, prayer. Bria and the rest of the Remnant held hands in a circle and prayed together.

"Lord, we come to you in power. We humbly ask you for victory over our enemies. Avenge those whose lives have been taken at the hands of Madam. Thank you Lord."

The Web members were impressed. They have never seen anything like that. They didn't know what to say so they just followed in silence. From the alley, they were able to see through the gate. One guard walked around the pool in the backyard. Teja told Bria that she wanted to get the first guard.

Bria said, "If you want this first guard, you will have to do it quietly. We don't want this to turn into some type of shootout."

Teja climbed the fence to the house next door. Her plan was to sneak up behind the guard and use her big knife to finish the job. At about the same time, Lacey has made it home. Madam had a short talk to her and released her like she promised. She ran to her door. She hasn't been home in a couple days. As soon as she made it into the house, she called Courtney.

Back at Madam's, Teja is waiting for the right moment to grab the guard. She stealthily hopped the fence. She pulled a double-edged dagger from her sleeve. She walked up behind the guard and showed no mercy. Teja grabbed her by her hair. She slit her throat and poked her in the heart and chest before pushing her body in the pool. Everyone was excited about her kill except Bria. Bria felt they were too excited about fighting and killing. Teja wiped of her dagger in the pool. She opened the gate and let everyone in. Christy had to find a way in so that she could disconnect the cameras.

### ###

Courtney has just received the call that she been waiting on all weekend. It was Lacey. She answered that phone as if her life depended on it.

"Hello Lacey?"

"Lacey replied, "It's me Courtney.

They both had their moment. They could not say a word to each other at first because their vocal chords were being drowned out by a fountain of tears.

Courtney replied, "Where you been Lacey, I needed you. They killed Janice and I was calling for you and you didn't answer me!"

"I apologize, Courtney. As soon as I heard the news about Janice, the next thing I know, I'm awakened by a cold bucket shower in Madams basement. I was looking for you too. I'm sorry to hear what happened to Janice."

Courtney talked while holding back her emotions, "How did you get home?"

"Madam just dropped me off."

Courtney anxiety kicked in. She remembered what Vanessa said about Shortie going to Madam house at sundown.

Shortie was living up to her word, they have made it into the house and disarmed the entire security system. There were more guards than expected. Two of the guards went outside to check the electrical panel. They had no idea what made the monitors stop working. Tiffany was on side of the house with Lisa at that time. Lisa pulled her gun out.

"Put that up. We have to be quiet so all the other guards won't be alerted," Tiffany added.

Lisa pulled out a sword and put her gun up.

She asked Tiffany, "Is this good enough?"

Tiffany replied, "What are you going to do with a big ass sword. You don't know how to use that."

Lisa replied, "Watch this."

As soon as the guards walked on side of the house, Lisa pushed Tiffany behind her. The guards saw them and pulled their guns. Lisa gripped the handle of the sword, took one step back and swung the sword in a figure 8 motion. The blade went across the arm of one and the wrist of the other. It freed the guns from them both. Lisa cut the main artery in one of the guards neck. The blood that squirted from her neck left Lisa blinded as it splattered in her face. She dropped the sword and started cleaning the blood off with her sleeve. The other guard ran towards the front of the house screaming for help. Tiffany immediately ran behind her. She tackled her in the front yard, pulled her dagger out and stabbed her. Two other guards saw her run from the side of the house. They drew their weapons. When Tiffany stood up, they fired their weapons at her. She ran back to the side of the house. Bria and Tonya heard the shots. While their attention was on Tiffany, Bria pulled her gun and shot one of them on the side of the head. Tonya ran and slid on the grass behind the second guard and cut her on back of the leg with her sword. She fell to the ground. Bria stood over her and shot her once in the chest.

### ###

After Courtney told Lacey of the plan that Shortie had, they both became anxious. They didn't want Shortie and the others to be hurt.

"Is their anyway to contact Shortie or anyone with them? Maybe we can stop them before Madam get there or something."

Courtney replied, "I don't have anyone's number, just Vanessa and she is at work."

"Did you say that she was a police officer?"

She shook her head, yes.

Lacey continued, "See can she drive her car by there."

Courtney agreed and called Vanessa. Lacey called Shae to see how far they were from the house.

By this time, Shortie and the others have searched the house and taken out all the guards. There was no sign of Madam or Natasha. They stood there disappointed. They knew that they didn't have many opportunities and these two attempts they came up empty handed. Shortie made sure that no one was injured. She told everyone to go ahead of her while she locked the gate. Bria led them back the same way they came.

Natasha drove down the long driveway.

Before she could make it down to the end of the driveway, Madam yelled, "Stop the damn car!"

She saw the three bodies laying on the front lawn. Shae phone rang but she ignored it. Her and Natasha got out the car and walked over to see what happened. Madam pulled her gun and walked to the back of the house. Shortie was having a difficult time locking the gate. Lisa saw that she was struggling.

"Bria, I will run and help Shortie real fast!"

Everyone waited as she ran down the alley. She was whispering to Shortie to hurry up as she walked towards her.

She told Lisa, "I will catch up with you'll. Go back Lisa, I got it."

Lisa stopped at a good distance back. Before she could turn around, she saw that Shortie lifted her head up and took a step backwards. Fem Madame put the gun to her chest and fired one shot. Shortie was hit. She fell to the ground and Lisa saw Madam step into the alley. She stood over her. Natasha stepped out behind her and shot her again. Lisa was in shock. She just stood there with her hand over her mouth.

Natasha looked up and they made eye contact. Lisa recognized her. Madam saw her silhouette but didn't know she was part of the Remnant. She lifted her gun and before she shot her, Natasha pushed her hand down.

"Put the gun away, you don't see the police lights in the front?"

The two of them met with the cops in the front yard. Shae was talking to them until Madam walked up.

"Can I help you officer?"

When Shae stepped out the way, Vanessa answered, "It has been reported that your neighbors heard gunshots."

"Officer, we just got home and we haven't heard any gun shots. Thanks for coming by and you have a good evening."

Vanessa looked around in awe. She could count three dead bodies laying on the front lawn. Her partner, the one that think she knows it all stepped out from behind the headlights. She approached Madam.

Vanessa thought to herself, "Sit your goofy ass down and shut the fuck up."

She greeted her with a hug, "Is everything good Madam."

Madam was so happy to see her.

"Anita, oh, I forgot, Officer Anita."

Vanessa found out that Anita and Shae are cousins. Anita turned to Vanessa and told her that their services are not needed. Vanessa heart was beating through her bullet proof vest. She cut the service lights out in the car. Once Anita finished talking, she got in the car. Vanessa started driving off. She looked in the rearview mirror and Madam and Natasha were waving. They rushed to the backyard and when they stepped in the alley, Shortie was gone.

"I want Shortie and her little ass crew, dead. I will go to the hotel downtown for a few days. Shae, go home. Natasha, get this shit cleaned up. Call me in a few days when it's done."